THE OTHERS

THE OTHERS

SARAH BLAU

Translated from the Hebrew by Daniella Zamir

MULHOLLAND BOOKS
LITTLE, BROWN AND COMPANY
NEW YORK BOSTON LONDON

The characters and events in this book are fictitious.
Any similarity to real persons, living or dead, is coincidental and
not intended by the author.

Mulholland Books / Little, Brown and Company
Hachette Book Group
1290 Avenue of the Americas, New York, NY 10104
mulhollandbooks.com

First English-language edition, April 2021
Published simultaneously in the UK by Pushkin Press
Originally published as האחרות by Kinneret in Israel, 2018

Mulholland Books is an imprint of Little, Brown and Company,
a division of Hachette Book Group, Inc. The Mulholland Books
name and logo are trademarks of Hachette Book Group, Inc.

ISBN 978-0-316-46087-3
LCCN 2020946135

Printing 1, 2021

LSC-C

Printed in the United States of America

In loving memory of
Uri Orbach

1

BY THE TIME that phone call from the police came, I was ready.

A gentle male voice asked if he could pop by for a quick questioning. That masculine energy threw me off for a moment. Rehearsing the scenario over and over, I had always imagined a woman, the kind with a gravelly, matter-of-fact voice. I always imagined her a bit tired, maybe after a long shift, most likely a mother. They always are.

And she would always react the same way, downright rattled by the gruesome murder, *gruesome and ritualistic, God, the horror!* Before pulling herself together and remembering why she had called me in the first place.

"Age?" she'd ask while typing. "Married? Kids?" And I'd reply to the two last questions with the usual "no," but this time with relief sweeping through my body.

No, ma'am, no kids.

According to the police report, Dina was murdered at 1 a.m.

The papers said it happened in "the dead of night," and catalogued all the grisly details, but the police report was worse – trust me.

The papers also said the victim was a professor of gender studies, and the murder was described as having "unique characteristics," by which they probably meant the fact that she was found hog-tied to a chair in her living room, the word "mother" carved into her forehead, and her dead hands clutching a baby doll.

What they didn't mention was that it was one of those reborn dolls you see on British TV shows featuring people with "peculiarities," who treat their dolls like real babies. These are usually after-hours shows, broadcast in "the dead of night," viewed by people like me with a curiosity tinged with horror. *I'm not going to become one of those people, right? I wouldn't rock a doll in a cradle and tell my guests, "Shush! He's having trouble sleeping," right?*

The doll found at the murder scene had a round face, puckered red lips and clear blue eyes with lifelike lashes.

What was mentioned was the struggle to pry the doll from the victim's hands. At first they thought it was rigor mortis, but then discovered the baby was glued to her. One sentimental journalist waxed poetic about how she looked like "a mother clinging to her infant, refusing to let go." Despite my best efforts, I couldn't imagine Dina clinging to anything, let alone an infant. *No, no, it had to have been glued to her.*

I guess Dina would have been pleased to know that her list of accomplishments extended over quite a few sentences. They cited the PhD she had obtained at such a young age, the dazzling lectures that drew packed audiences and the brilliant essays, highlighting, of course, the one about childfree women in the Bible, the one that had cemented her status as "one of the most prominent and polemical feminist theorists of our times." They also noted that she had chosen neither to marry nor to have children, and had become a leading advocate for this "controversial movement."

They did not mention the resistance of her skin during the attempts to yank the doll out of her hands, resulting in her having to be buried along with it, the doll pressed up against her.

And I couldn't help but think, *There you have it, Dina, you're finally a mother.*

2

My falling-out hair is gathered in clumps in the corners of every room.

The whole apartment is filled with boxes and hairballs. I keep tripping over the former and stepping on the latter. There's your usual hair loss, the one women's magazines will subtly refer to as "normal from a certain age," and there's the other kind, a product of my own pulling and yanking. At least I don't swallow it. Every now and then I'll stumble over an article about a giant hairball surgically removed from the stomach of some neurotic young woman, and in the photo accompanying the article, it always looks like a hairy baby monster.

I still think about Maor's parting remark before leaving, "Your hair is all over the house, do something about it, it's gross." *Bam!* The door slams shut, kicking up a tiny hairball past my face.

For the first time in my life, I considered swallowing it.

I'm sweeping the apartment with a new silicone broom; I bought it yesterday, dragging it with me all the way home, attracting the curious gazes of passers-by, as if they expected me to ride it. They should be grateful it's a shiny, sterile silicone broom and not the giant straw witch one I got for fancy dress at Purim. Although, it is possible that no one was actually looking at me and that I was merely imagining the scrutinizing stares, and even more likely that it was just that damn guilt following me around like a gloomy companion.

The apartment is full of dust; I cough and my eyes well up. My image in the mirror seems too flushed and dishevelled. Not good. I have to look calm and collected for the visit; the detective might have sounded young, but not stupid.

Most importantly, I have to stop with the remarks that come pouring out of me when I get nervous; sometimes I think it's momentary fits of Tourette's. Otherwise there's no explaining why, when the detective sensitively enquires whether I've been feeling afraid since the murder, with all the frenzied fuss kicked up around childless women, that instead of muttering a feeble yes, I feel compelled to share that "The scariest thing about this whole business is that they finally made a mother out of her."

No, the silence on the other end of the line did not bode well.

A brief knock on the door and in he comes, almost tripping on one of the boxes I failed to move aside in time, and now he's smiling awkwardly while reaching out for a handshake.

He's young. Unreasonably young, with that boyish smile that brings a dimple to his left cheek, just like Maor's dimple. Like Maor he's carpeted in fine stubble, and those bright eyes, just like Maor's, study you to reach private conclusions he has no intention of sharing.

Oh, yes, it's definitely there, the resemblance, especially in the particular green of their eyes, and the lashes that go on forever, and the crooked smile aware of its effect on you.

This time it's a real resemblance, not the imagined kind right after a break-up, when every man (including the old broom salesman) looks like a doppelgänger of the absconding lover. *Don't go there, Sheila, be smart.*

"Pleased to meet you, I'm Micha," he says, his hand still suspended mid-air. I notice a tattoo of a sentence in thin Rashi script across the tender part of his wrist. I can't read it, but I don't need to in order to make my observation: erstwhile prince of the religious Boy Scouts. In my mind's eye I see the absent kipah resting atop his head, the excessive self-confidence making up for a late-blooming masculinity.

"Moving out?" he casually enquires while sitting down on the freed-up part of the couch, his eyes casting about, studying the contents of the open boxes.

"Just moved in," I reply while we both simultaneously catch sight of the small baby doll poking out of the box behind the door. *You idiot!*

"Still playing with dolls?" The light-hearted tone doesn't fool me. His eyes are devouring the doll, its one eye closed and the other looking straight ahead with an icy blue stare. It looks like someone punched her.

"A gift from my ex," I reply. "Sort of a joke."

"And what does it mean? The expectation of a baby together?"

A baby? Dream on, Sherlock.

"Not exactly," I say, dragging out the words. "More of a joke about him being a baby."

"Well, most women think all men are babies."

And there it is again – his Boy Scout guide's smile, instantly delivering me back to my days as enamoured Girl Scout, because some patterns are so deeply ingrained in us that we immediately fall back into them, like eternal roleplay, and your part never changes, no matter who you are or how old, because the role was tailor-made for you from day one.

"He really was a baby," I explain. "Only twenty-six."

"Huh, nearly my age."

And already he regrets sharing this information, but his mind starts racing, doing the math, because if Dina and I were in college together, that means I'm at least how old… ? His mind is busy calculating, his eyes sweeping over me and that mouth quietly mumbling a few polite words that whiz right past me… Because I instantly recognized that wandering gaze of his, and I know all too well what's running through his mind. I know that if he wasn't on the job right now, he'd already be informing me that he too had dated an "older woman," because they all do at some point, especially the cute ex-Orthodox hotties, and it always ended "not so well, but we're still on friendly terms." Pfff. But he wouldn't say that, would he? He's here to try to glean information about the murder from the victim's best friend – former best friend – isn't he? And he seems like someone who can watch his mouth.

"I had a relationship with an older woman too."

Well, well! You do surprise, kid, although I'm not so sure you did in fact date an "older woman," because a real older woman would have taught you not to call her that, a real older woman would have had your dumb, pretty head if she heard you talking about her that way. Obviously, you would have had to pretend you're both the same age, and if you accidentally let a wayward *mum* slip, you had to immediately laugh it off, *I was just kidding, Mum.*

"I mean, not *older*," he rushes to correct himself, "just older than me. She was about your age, thirty-something?"

Okay, stupid he ain't.

"I'm forty-one." You'll be forty-two next month, and you know that; each year counts, and you know that too.

"So my girlfriend was your age."

Hmm… he isn't backing out, interesting. I wonder whether this is some kind of manipulation, to butter me up to get the information he wants, but that attentive gaze is still there, and so is that soft-looking, beautiful mop of hair. On the other hand, we haven't exchanged a single word about the murder. But that dimple won't stop flashing in front of me, followed by that smile that's making me weak in the knees again, so much so that I feel myself melting, fading away, lowering my eyes to the tattoo on his delicate wrist and asking, "Did it hurt?"

"Like hell."

"Anything to drink?" Go to the kitchen before you make a huge mistake, go, remove yourself from his presence.

"I'd love some coffee," he says, just when I remember I have nothing to offer but tepid tap water with a distinct metallic tang – a taste I have yet to acquire. I serve him the water in a sticky glass, which he studies at length.

"Don't worry, everything's kosher here." I can't help myself.

"It doesn't bother me," he replies with a curious gaze. "It's been years since I bothered myself with such things."

"I have a sophisticated ex-Orthodox radar," I explain, an answer that usually satisfies them.

"You're the first person to be on to me this quickly," he admits.

"Really?" I ask, even though I'm not surprised. "It's so obvious, it's like the kipah is still on your head."

And he reaches out, not to the top of his head to check if it has sprouted a kipah, but to the box behind the door, from which he pulls out the small baby doll. Am I imagining it, or has its closed eye opened slightly?

"You know, this doll looks a lot like the one glued to Dina Kaminer's hands," he says without looking at me.

"I didn't glue anything to anyone, if that's what you're insinuating."

Bad answer. Very bad answer, because now he's peering at me with that scrutinizing gaze, the one I've been worrying about from the moment he stepped into my apartment.

You idiot.

"If you haven't noticed, I didn't ask you if you glued anything," he says. "I haven't even asked you where you were two weeks ago on Wednesday at 10 p.m." His voice is very quiet.

"Wednesday at 10 p.m.?" *10 p.m.!*

"One of the neighbours had just stepped outside and heard Dina opening the door to her apartment and saying to someone, 'I'm glad you came,' but she could barely make out the voice of the person who replied. She's almost convinced it was a woman, but…"

"But that doesn't fit the profile of the anti-feminist-anti-childfree-woman murderer you people built," I say.

"Good observation," he says and courageously sips his water, pretending it's not revolting. "So how about I ask you now where you were Wednesday at 10 p.m.? Would that be okay?"

And once again he flashes that smile of his, all too aware of its effect on me. With an expression both innocent and smug he leans back on the couch when a grating squeak suddenly sounds from underneath him, and he leaps up, spilling his water onto his trousers.

The damn doll! Her face, now squished, sends me a mocking smile.

Before he leaves he'll get to hear that on Wednesday evening I was home watching TV, "without a shred of an alibi, but it's a known fact that the biggest criminals always have the best alibis." He'll nod in agreement, ask about my relationship with Dina during our college days, hear how "we weren't in contact at all in recent years, you know how it is, life just took us down different roads," a line uttered in such a convincing tone I'd almost believe it myself; a few more dimple-revealing smiles. A few more of my attempts not to stare at the wet spot on his trousers, a few more gazes I'd never imagine I'd receive from the long and oh-so-young arm of the law, and that's that, we're already at the door.

He stands close to me, almost leaning in. I feel that magnetic field created between two people whose mere acquaintanceship will lead to disaster, and I shudder.

"So now what?" I ask.

"This is when I tell you that if you recall anything that might be of any help, call me." He's very close right now.

"Ah. This isn't when you tell me I can't leave town?" Something about his look just begs for wisecracks.

"I've seen those detective shows too," he says. "And besides, you already skipped town."

Another one of those nostril-flaring smiles, another brushing of his hand over his soft, thick hair, and he turns to leave. The door slamming behind him sends a tiny hairball hurling right into my mouth; I spit it out and hear the familiar giggle, *dumb baby*. The voice is Dina's.

3

HE WAS RIGHT, obviously, the fledgling detective. I left Tel Aviv in the nick of time.

Too many women like me have walked the streets there – all of us good-looking, polished and prim, clever, sharp-edged, hovering like butterflies and prickly like a fertility-test needle, all of us ticking time bombs, *tick-tock, tick-tock, no tot, no tot.*

Last week, during a lecture called "Childfree by Choice: Women without Children," held at a bar in Tel Aviv, a doll was tossed into the crowded room; it was one of those cheap, ugly ones, without eyelashes. It was naked, and the words "Mummy dearest" were written in red ink on its forehead. Once the hysteria died down, virtually every woman in the bar took a photo of the little dolly and posted it on her Facebook page, along with a withering indictment of police incompetence.

The perps were caught two days later, two boys who were so worked up about the ritualistic murder, about the growing frenzy and mostly, by their own admission, "about the possibility that finally we have a serious, creative killer in Israel," that they decided to pitch in with their efforts. In the newspaper photo they looked like a couple of Moomins, soft and spongy, and I wondered which of the two had undressed the doll. I'd put my money on the ugly one.

*

And Dina was there, everywhere you looked there was Dina, or rather, Dr Kaminer – in those flattering profile pieces, with heavy-handed hints about her private life (under the guise of investigative journalism), in the eulogies by her colleagues and in the familiar press photos. They kept publishing the one in which she was caught grinning, looking ruddy and wild, her smile – revealing the gap between her front teeth – slightly silly, and more than anything, very out of character.

I have no doubt that if she were still alive, she'd be calling the editor to demand a more appropriate photo, and her demands would be met. She was a master of the art of persuasion: aggressive and charismatic, used to getting her way. *But none of that helped her in the end, did it?*

That particular article was also dredged up. One of the newspapers reprinted it, verbatim, and I photographed it and turned the image into my screensaver.

I noticed that the people who quoted from the article hadn't actually read it, but merely regurgitated the same inane assumptions that appeared in the papers without variation. "Did the women in the Bible actually choose to be childfree? Could it be that Dr Kaminer encouraged women not to give birth? Should childless women be afraid to walk the streets now? Could our women be in danger? Could it be? Could it??" and more and more could-it-bes, all similarly poorly phrased, and not one able to hide its smugness.

Tick-tock, tick-tock, no tot, no tot.

A radio host tried to rev up his listeners with the survey question, "Who would you turn into a mother?" He was suspended immediately, of course, but not before suggesting a few interesting options, including a famous actress who stated she wasn't interested in having children, a female director who spoke out against childbirth and an emerging young singer who, in her very first interview, announced she had no intention of becoming a mother.

While reading those three interviews, I already knew that within three years all three women would be smiling at us from magazine covers holding their bundles of joy below the identical caption: "Motherhood has changed me."

Because by now I know that if you're not interested in having children, you don't go announcing it to the world like that. It's something private and profound, which slowly boils in the depths of your consciousness before simmering to the surface, and even then it won't stop fighting you till your very last egg dries up – I should know.

"Little witch, little witch fell down a ditch. Come out and play! she cried all day. But no one did, and in the ditch she hid..."

I rush to the window to peek outside, and can't believe kids still sing that. A few children are standing in a circle around a chubby little girl sprawled on the ground with a scraped knee, chanting at the top of their lungs, repeating the words over and over again. The girl in the middle is confused, not sure whether to laugh or cry. I'd advise her to cry.

I slam the window shut and pieces of plaster come flying off the crumbling wall. It's the window facing Ramat Gan, a city east of Tel Aviv. The windows on the other side of the apartment offer completely different vistas.

This apartment that I have moved back into is located on a curious spot on the map: right on the dividing line between

Israel's ultra-Orthodox epicentre and one of its many nondescript secular cities, an area commonly known as "Bnei Brak bordering Ramat Gan." Usually it serves as a code name for the residents of Bnei Brak who are more reticent about their background, in which case they'll say: "I live in Bnei Brak but on the border of Ramat Gan," even if they live dead in the middle of Rabbi Akiva Street, which is nowhere near Ramat Gan.

But my apartment really is located in between, so when I'm asked "Where are you from?", I give whatever answer will serve me best. Efraim, the director of the Bible Museum, who finds the fact that I'm religious – even if only tenuously – a hot commodity, will get the answer "Bnei Brak," while the occasional taxi driver, all too willing to dole out his opinions about synagogue and state, will get the aloof answer: "Ramat Gan." An answer made to measure. And in general, it's not bad for a girl to slightly blur her past. I should know.

And there's another advantage, a secret one.

Whenever I feel the youth draining from my body, feel it on my desiccating skin, my period cut another day shorter, the subtle-yet-palpable slackening of my facial muscles, the bristly hairs sprouting from the tip of my chin, in short, whenever I start doubting my feminine allure, I'll go moseying along the streets of Bnei Brak, where one always feel lusted after with all those disapproving gazes and reproachful twitches. The slightest bit of cleavage or a skirt cut even an inch above the knee will give you the feeling that you're Lilith the seductress. It's a potent youth potion, downright magic.

Maor hated the fact that I was a former Bnei Brak girl; the city seemed inferior and run down to him. When he heard I was planning to move back there, he grimaced, couldn't understand how I could give up living in Tel Aviv. Even when I explained that I was presented with the opportunity to live almost rent-free in an apartment that belonged to a relative, he shrugged. "It would really bum me out to visit you there," he said.

I guess it really bummed him out. It must have – we broke up even before the move transpired.

I study the pug-faced doll he gave me back then, during the early glory days of our budding romance, when everything gleamed with promise. I should have seen it for the ominous sign it was. When your boyfriend jokes about the considerable age gap between you, it's going to end in tears and they're going to be yours.

It's true that I told him right off the bat that I wasn't interested in having kids, both because it was the truth and because I wanted to clear that sinister cloud that turns every woman in her late thirties into an intimidation.

He replied that neither was he – *a lie! They're always interested, especially the more selfish ones among them* – and he stuck to it for a long time, until he once asked, "Hypothetically, if you did want a kid, who would you have it with?" I, whose sole intention was to compliment him, immediately blurted, "Only with you, my love," which of course produced precisely the opposite effect. His eyes turned into dark pools of fear. I think that's when our relationship's countdown timer started ticking. *Tick-tock.*

And now, sitting in my rocking chair the next day in the empty apartment like an idiot, I'm holding an ugly doll and waiting for a call from Maor's deadly double. Maor's deadly *policeman* double.

Every object in the apartment is screaming at you to watch out, but you're not listening. The walls are boring into you, watching you waiting for the phone to ring, hovering around the device with that hungry expression while the apartment slowly fills with a familiar sensation. It's called anticipation, and it's disgusting.

I'm supposed to be glad that I got rid of him so easily, he's no fool, that Micha, so I'm supposed to be pleased that he went on his merry way without asking the hard questions, supposed to lock the door behind him and spin into a little happy dance. So why the hell am I staring at the phone screen, checking that my battery is still alive? Why can't I concentrate on anything other than that crazed buzzing in my head? *Why? Because you're a brainless baby, that's why.*

At least good old Google is still waiting for me with open, gift-bearing arms.

I retype "Dina Kaminer" and wait for the deluge of results. No new hits since the last time I checked (an hour ago), no new suspects, no interesting new theories, and the phony concern (with just a touch of *Schadenfreude*) for the welfare of the city's single women has been replaced by a few preachy articles about the damage women who keep putting off the decision to have kids are causing themselves blah-blah-blah. In other words, no useful information. I scroll down to the bottom, where the dark world of internet commenters is revealed before me.

It's incredible how much they hate her. Even like this – murdered, violated, stripped of her dignity and titles – even now they hate her. *They always hated her.*

And what's that? A new article. The headline is sentimental – "Dr Dina Kaminer – the mother of all those who do not wish to be mothers" – not bad, kind of poetic, I'm not sure what Dina would have thought about it, but I find there's a certain beauty to it. The article was written by one of her research colleagues, and the comments inform me that she too is childless. They're on a downright rampage of wrath and contempt, from comments like "fuglies like you shouldn't have kids," *classic*, to "who would even want to have kids with a selfish raggedy hag with a stick up her fat arse," *slightly banal, the usual displays of verbal diarrhoea*, and there's also the tasteful suggestion: "You should find someone who'll inseminate you and along with his semen maybe pump a little sense into your sterile brains."

Oh, well, some things never change.

None of these birdbrain commenters has my way with words.

Now, obviously, I wouldn't dare write a single syllable; I have no intention of letting some police prodigy connect certain dots that could get me into trouble, but in the past, oh, I definitely wrote a comment or two.

Because unlike these Neanderthals with their predictable and limited scopes of knowledge, I knew Dina and knew just where to strike. I knew where it really hurt. *Sheila, you little witch.*

In one of her interviews, when she spoke about how "the verbal aggression displayed by internet commenters is owed to their anonymity," I realized she was on to me; I kept on reading and discovered several other sharpened arrows aimed specifically at me. But I didn't care, at that point my hatred towards her was far beyond reason.

You see, I hated everything that had to do with her. The passive-aggressiveness that was really just aggressiveness, the dark oily hair she kept in a bun, her bulging, black cow eyes, the giant breasts she carried with the arrogance of a battleship, her self-righteousness, but more than anything, I hated her voice, deep and purring, a velvety voice that belied the steely punch.

That's exactly how she sounded that Wednesday evening, when she opened the door and said to me, "I'm glad you came."

4

"But you didn't kill her, right?" Only Eli could produce such a sentence so matter-of-factly and calmly.

"And don't tell me I sound like a bad thriller," he adds, reading my mind, as always.

I sit in front of him in his office, the day after the police visit, drinking from his Coke can without giving it a second thought. Eli's office is my safe space, Eli himself is my safe space, this faithful, doglike friend. (Actually, he looks more like a hamster. A tall hamster, a handsome hamster, some might even say attractive hamster, but still, we're talking hamster here.) And if only I was able to fall in love with him, I would be the happiest woman alive. No, that's not right, I would obviously be an entirely different person, a person who could fall in love with Eli. Regretfully – I am not that person.

He's pleasant, Eli, and smart, and his mere presence has a calming effect on me. He's also patient and has been able to read my mind with uncanny accuracy over the years, but as you've probably figured out by now, that's not the particular set of traits that attracts me in a man. *Tick-tock, tick-tock.*

Eli was the one who helped me realize, after hours of conversation, that a major part of my unfortunate attraction to young men lies in the fact that everything is still open before them, still shiny and fresh, even if they don't end up pursuing any of their options – the power lying in the very promise is overwhelming. With Eli, for instance, just looking at him I can tell exactly how his life (or our shared life) would look in twenty years, down to the returns on our taxes, which obviously he'd fill out himself. On top of his many virtues, Eli is also the accountant for the museum I work for, *but even an office romance isn't quite exciting enough for you, huh?*

About three years ago, after a night of bad dreams featuring all the ghosts of my past, I woke up frightened and dazed and fixed my eyes on the mirror to discover a bristly black hair sticking out from my chin. At that precise moment, the most pointless sentence in the Hebrew language popped into my mind: "Why not give it a try?"

Why not give Eli a try, Sheila? Why do you have to be that way? He's been devoted to you for such a long time, and it's not impossible that somewhere, deep inside you, there's some kernel of attraction. After all, whenever he tells you he started dating someone, you feel the icy fist tightening around your heart, and you just can't wait for the budding romance to shrivel and die, right?

I promised myself that when we next met I'd look at Eli as a serious object of desire, and somehow managed to stoke myself with such romantic ideations that I couldn't wait to see him. Unfortunately, Eli, utterly in the dark about his new object-of-desire status, showed up in frayed brown slippers, and when I approached him, the smell they gave off was so repulsive that I instantly and permanently gave up all the "why not give it a try" fantasies.

It was only a few days later that I recalled that Eli wore those slippers often and never before had I given any thought to their particular aroma, so I must have ordered my subconscious to find him repulsive no matter what, and the said subconscious, obedient as ever – mainly to my self-destructive orders – simply honed in on the first thing it found.

Eli sips from the can without saying a word about my having nearly drunk it dry. It clinks against his teeth.

"I want to understand something," he says, "did someone see you arrive at Dina's on the night of the murder?"

"God, no," I reply. "If that were the case I'd be busted by now, but apparently someone heard her opening the door for me."

"At 7 p.m.? That detective told you it happened at 10." I notice the slight change of tone when he says "that detective."

"True, but that busybody might have gotten the time wrong."

"Sheila, you know perfectly well nosy neighbours never get anything wrong."

He's right, of course, anyone who's ever read a detective novel knows there is no one more in-the-know than the nosy neighbour. *And no one more dangerous.*

I tell him more about Micha's visit without offering too many details, since I know Eli has it all figured out before I've even opened my mouth. He doesn't ask any questions, knowing he'll eventually hear more than he bargained for.

There's only one thing that bothers him. "Dina called and initiated the meeting herself?" he asks. "After all these years? After everything that happened?"

"Yes."

"So how come she wanted to meet all of a sudden?"

I sink into my chair, unable to bring myself to tell him how it all went wrong, how such terrible things were said, things that are painful just to think about, and how, after all these years, she still had the capacity to hurt me. *And you honed your capacity to hurt her, so stop whining. You're the one who's still breathing.*

"So how are you? It's been years!"

More than a decade and a half, dear, but who's counting. I give her the once-over, disappointed to find that her photos in the papers hadn't been retouched and that she really does look terrific, with all that black hair, the regal forehead and big dark eyes. In college they used to say we looked alike, and back then it was sort of true, but the marks life has left on us removed any resemblance: she looks sated and smug while I project a kind of constant hunger. But at least she seems to have put on a few pounds, crossed that fine line from curvy to chubby. *Goody.*

We consider each other, locking eyes like a couple of gunslingers. I'm the first to avert my gaze, and it lands on a wall covered with shiny diplomas and certificates of appreciation. And there's also that one picture I know well, of a figure I know well, *all too well*, I can't help myself and read the caption aloud, slowly, "Miriam the prophetess."

"It's not the same picture," she blurts out.

"Obviously," I reply. We both know what happened to the original picture, and neither of us is bent on bringing it up. The picture from that night. The image of young Dina suddenly flits before me, hair dishevelled, big eyes gaping wide, face flushed with excitement, white knuckles clenching the tambourine, pounding on it with all her might, like the palpitations of a big, angry heart, *Thrump, thrump, thrump!*

"You still play the drums?" I ask and can't believe that question came out of my mouth, and before I had even taken a seat in one of her lustrous white armchairs. I must hate her more than I thought.

"I quit," she replies, and judging by her tone I can assume when. I collapse into one of the armchairs by the woolly carpet, also white. *Without a single child here to change that.*

"Coffee?" Her voice pleasant once more. I once read that hosts feel more at ease when their guests accept their offers to wine and dine you, something to do with mechanisms of control and conciliation.

"Sure," I reply and instantly regret it. *Why please that bitch?*

"I only have soy milk."

"That's fine," I say.

"You know they say it's loaded with hormones," she says, while pouring it into two coffee cups. Her hands around the mugs seem tiny. I forgot how small they were compared to the rest of her, with almond-shaped pink nails; it's the only part of her body that looks vulnerable. All Kaminers have those tiny hands. I recall that time her brother placed his on my shoulder; it was at a Purim party and excusable by the fact that we were all slightly buzzed. His touch was incredibly light, spine-tingling and oddly pleasurable; it was the first time any man had ever put his hand on me and I told him that. He didn't remove it, and we stayed like that for some time. But after the party I never saw him again. I guess Dina was on guard. There could have been thousands of reasons why she didn't want her brother to start dating me, but I was interested in the real one.

We sip our coffee in silence.

"At least it tastes better now," she says. "Remember the disgusting soy milk at college?"

Do I ever. I remember Ronit with her lactose intolerance, always having to add canned soy milk to her coffee. I once accidentally took a sip of her coffee, and to this day I can still feel the awful aftertaste in my mouth, like the liquid that pools at the bottom of a can of mushrooms.

"Are you still in contact with Ronit?" she asks casually. She must have experienced a similar recollection.

"No," I reply with the same blasé manner. "You?"

She shoots a quick glance at the picture of Miriam, and once again I recall the last time we all met, vividly remember the sound of the tambourine, its beat. How did we fail to notice it was an entirely different rhythm, dark and thick? *Thrump, thrump! Blood, blood, the end will come, little hands will never drum!*

"I see her every now and then, on the occasional panel," Dina says, and my mouth instantly fills with the taste of canned mushrooms. Bitter.

Ronit, the third member of our special group – *special and then some!* – had become an actress. She may not have broken into the top league of actresses in the country, but she has found enough success to pinch my jealous heart. I resent her for her humble achievements, and of course blame Dina for that too.

"You're still giving lectures at the Bible Museum?" She surprises me.

"How do you know I work there?"

"A few years ago they asked me to give a lecture there, and the director told me you work in my field."

Her field! For a moment I consider slamming my mug in her face, just hard enough to graze that high forehead, just to wipe that complacency off her face. But I wouldn't dare, of course, *you never did have the courage!* Look at us, so civil and pleasant towards each other, sitting here with legs crossed, she with her perfectly filed manicure, me with my hooves, talking like the polite, good friends we once were. And we were friends, weren't we? She did refuse to come lecture at the museum, didn't she? At least she has the sensitivity not to rub her success in my face.

"Your director barely agreed to pay a quarter of my usual fee," she says. *Sensitivity, my arse.*

"He also sounded like a fuddy-duddy from hell," she adds.

As always, her observation is spot on.

Efraim, the museum director, was indeed a horrible Conservadox. It seemed as if he dedicated most of his life to battling feminist scholars who tried to desecrate the sanctity of his museum. Since a sizeable portion of the museum's budget relied on donations from the US, and since a few snappy liberal ladies sat on the board, he had no choice but to display goodwill and open-mindedness to "all movements and denominations." When donors visited, he'd ask me to conduct the tour and to give free rein to all my subversive ideas, which would normally make him itch all over. But I guess Dina was more than he could bear, since she never gave that lecture.

"At the time I thought it could actually be interesting to bump into each other," she says.

Yes. Interesting indeed.

"I never understood why you went and buried yourself in that dinky museum." She takes another sip of her soy-milk coffee, pumping hormones right into her bloodstream, sitting in front of me bloated and glistening, smug and self-satisfied, looking like a heifer about to calve.

"*You* never understood?" I say, barely finding the strength to speak.

"Yes," she carries on, "after all, you were brilliant, you had real strokes of genius. I thought you'd break into the big leagues, like me."

She leans back, sliding her arse further into the *white* armchair, her small hands still wrapped around her mug. My hands, in contrast, ball into fists. Wanting to injure, but once again failing to work up the nerve. Because what could I possibly tell her? That my biggest stroke of genius was stolen from me? I still remember the shock that ripped through me when I saw that seminal article in the journal. The title was "The Childfree Women of the Bible," and it caused a fiery wave to wash over me. Horror, shock, surprise, and yes, there was even pride there, I was foolish enough to feel proud of the puny acknowledgement she threw my way at the bottom of the article: "For the inspiration." *I'll show her inspiration!*

But I don't say a word, not yet, and neither does she, studying my face with mocking scrutiny, searching for something she won't find, probably knowing I won't dare come out and say it, just as I didn't then or during the many years since.

And it's not as if I wasn't urged to do something, to say something, for heaven's sake! Eli headed the persuasion campaign. "You have to call her and demand an explanation, or at least more serious credit," he kept imploring, but I refused. It's hard to understand, but I couldn't bring myself to call her, even to imagine the scenario. (Back then, I mean. Over time the image of me screaming at her on the phone, demanding justice, has become frayed around the edges, worse for wear.)

It's possible that was ground zero. Yes, there. My inability to face her swelled into an inability to face the world. It was easier to choose avoidance, that slow drifting towards "que sera, sera," everything slipping through my fingers. But in this life, when you avoid one thing, another (usually revolting) one will come take its place.

And that revolting thing is now sitting in front of me, bloated with satisfaction, wanting to say something but unable to because it's licking from its tiny fingers the white cream filling from a pack of Oreos that has somehow eluded me. It's sucking its fingers now, this disgusting thing.

"Maybe I didn't make the big leagues," I raise my voice, "because some bitch stole my best idea and turned it into an article."

She blinks at the word bitch.

"I wouldn't call it *stealing*," she says after some thought.

"Oh, no? So what would you call it?"

"Come on, Sheila, we hung in a group, were together 24–7, you know how it is, ideas get around. Someone came up with the idea that even back in biblical times, it was possible some women didn't want to become mothers, and I took it from there."

"*Someone* came up with the idea?"

"Fine, it was you," she replies and sips her coffee, a giant gulp that sounds like a burp. "But I gave you credit, didn't I? I thanked you, told everyone it was an idea I came up with together with a college friend."

"Who even notices the stupid acknowledgements?" I get up, my feet sinking into the soft white carpet, *forever white*. "You robbed me, Dina, and you know it! And that's not even the worst thing you did, and we both know that."

There. I said it.

"Oh, so now you're going to blame me for everything?" She kept her voice low, and that made the words sting all the more. "You're going to blame me for being stuck in some crummy museum no one's heard of, getting a measly two hundred shekels for some half-arsed lecture about Sarah the matriarch? You're going to pin that on me too?"

She's still sitting there, arse-deep in the armchair, while I stand in front of her. The picture of Miriam on the wall before me, my ears pounding with the beat of the tambourine, *Thrump, thrump! Thrump, thrump!* Only this time it's war drums, having been silenced for too long.

"You stole my idea, you always stole from me, robbed me of much more than an article. You stole from all of us, from Ronit, from Naama!"

I know the mention of Naama's name will shut her up. And indeed, she blinks again, doesn't dare take another sip of coffee, sitting completely still with sticky fingers, staring ahead. I know exactly what's going through her mind, who's going through her mind, the corpse exhumed and put on display here on the white carpet.

Unfortunately, Dina could never be silenced for long. She slowly gets up, with her usual air of gravitas, buttocks swaying as she approaches me.

"Now you listen to me," she says in a tone somewhere between threatening and consoling, "I did you a favour, Sheila, we both know you wouldn't have done a thing with your half-baked idea, but I sat and researched and wrote and actualized and coincidentally happened to do you the biggest favour anyone has ever done. Now you have someone to blame, an address for all your failures! Must be nice, loser!"

I stare at her in disbelief. *Loser?*

I can't believe we've sunk so low – *loser?* That the mask of politeness has been ripped off so quickly; why do we even bother keeping up appearances if they shatter so easily? *Loser!*

I guess Dina was thinking the same thing, because now she pulls herself together, hands balling into fists, wants to say something but decides against it. She returns to her chair and then slowly leans forward, reaching for her mug, wanting to take a sip, or at least draw the mug to her lips, but the cup is see-through and we can both see it's empty.

She tucks a loose strand behind her ear – *what thick, lush hair! How does a woman her age have such luxuriant hair?* And I notice her hand is shaking.

"Look," she says, "this is really not what I meant to happen when I initiated this get-together, I just..." She searches for words. "Let's behave like adults, we're too old to sling mud at each other. It reminds me of an article I once read that people without children preserve some infantile aspect within them, and I think we both proved that just now, acting like two little girls." She smiles, and it's her regular, self-assured smile again.

And that smile, the familiar smile of that twenty-year-old student, shatters before me, and Dina, unaware of what's going on inside me, proceeds to wax poetic that "It's awfully biblical what just happened here, truly primal, how for a moment we were like two biblical characters fighting over a birthright... it reminds me of an article I've been wanting to write about core essences, imprinted in our DNA."

And she holds forth, unfolding the biblical analogy her mind has conceived, as if she has already forgotten those terrible words uttered only moments ago... she is already someplace else, immersed in her idea, and I realize that everything that has just transpired between us barely touched her, not really, *because she doesn't care, don't you get it? She never did, you're the one whose soul has been scorched by every article she published*, and you kept waging this ancient battle inside you, always saying one day, one day... but the day has come, and here she is, sitting in front of you, arse planted in the armchair, and you, as always, a flat-out *loser*, the kind that keeps her mouth shut while letting the Dina Kaminers of the world piss on her head.

"So you're going to teach me the Bible now, Dina?"

My voice sounds wet and ugly even to me. "Maybe it's time I teach you something? Something for you to steal for your new article? And I'm saying here and now that you can keep all the credit, happily, are you listening?" Oh, yes, she's definitely listening. "So my idea for essences imprinted in the DNA goes something like this – just like they went and fucked our biblical Dina, you went and fucked me, deep and hard, how do you like that analogy?"

No, it wasn't easy for me to come out with the "fucked," but it was worth it. Her mouth was agape with surprise. I knew my vulgarity would shut her up. Vulgarity always had that effect on her. That's just how it is; when little religious girls hear the word "fuck," they clam up real fast. Even I need a moment to compose myself.

Dina is still silent, then she gets up, goes to the fridge, pours herself a glass of water and gulps it down, then comes back into the living room and takes another Oreo, licks her lips and bites into it peacefully, her gaze resting on the picture on the wall, and the corners of her mouth start curling into a smile. *That smile!*

"You know what, Dina? I hope you drop dead."

My voice is hushed, but it doesn't take more than that. That old fear sparks in her eyes.

5

I RUSH BY the wax pavilion, following my conversation with Eli, ignoring the figurines' inquisitive eyes. I'm not in the mood.

Last night I tossed and turned in bed, replaying my meeting with Dina, knowing there was something that eluded me there, something important. Some word that was said, a clue suspended mid-air, something deep and dark, impalpable, like BO.

A moment before falling asleep, my body already cold and slack, I felt the answer teetering on the edge of my consciousness, like when you're about to sneeze, but the fleeting moment passes, *it's right under your nose, silly!*

The figurines lock their wax eyes on me, none of them smiling.

The collection was donated by one of our bigger benefactors abroad. At first there were a few who tried to object on the grounds of "Thou shalt not make unto thee any graven image," and there was a vociferous article in the local paper and an attempt to organize a protest against "blasphemous" sculptures "in the Bible museum no less!" But as always in such cases, when it comes to a serious benefactor, the collection stayed right where it was. Normally, I actually like walking along the pavilion, but these days are anything but normal, and the figurines look especially grouchy.

Our mother Leah seems grouchiest of all, with those dead

eyes of hers, placed next to a figurine of our father Jacob, and her big brood of kids are all slung from her arms like cherries on melting ice cream. The artist obviously took his interpretation of "tender eyes" a little too far, rendering her expression a unique combination of cross-eyed and blind.

Our mother Sarah, standing by the figurine of our father Abraham, also frowns at me, looking old and more wrinkled than ever, especially since she's holding the little wax hand of baby Isaac. Sarah's Egyptian slave Hagar, of course, has been sculpted as young and beautiful, "too beautiful," a visitor once remarked disapprovingly. I agreed with her, finding her generous and perky wax breasts annoying as well.

As usual, I pick up my pace as I pass by the figurine of Miriam the prophetess, feeling that same old peevishness over the fact that they chose to immortalize her in her famous scene, as a little girl peeking through the reeds, looking over baby Moses, who, for some reason, was shaped as a pig in a blanket. At least he got another figurine as an adult, while Miriam has been frozen in time as an anxious child. What about the powerful prophetess she grew up to be? What about it, indeed.

Today I rush past her even faster than usual, a few more figurines and I'll be out of the pavilion. Here's David and his wives, a smug redhead surrounded by a group of beautiful women, and next to them, at some distance, sits a proud, sad woman, her small crown atilt. All the other women are carrying a chubby wax toddler in their arms, while she settles for the crown and a hungry expression. It's Michal, daughter of Saul, the only one among King David's wives I was ever partial to. But the lecture about her is in scarce demand, or as some instructional coordinator from the South once commented to me, "Who wants to hear about that barren hag?" before asking to sign up for the lecture "Four Mothers – Birthing a Proud Nation."

Adam and Eve are waiting for me near the exit, clad head to toe in fig leaves.

Efraim saw to that, brought kids over for a special arts and crafts workshop to churn out dozens of ornate fig leaves, and glued them on himself. I remember watching him, gluing on one leaf after another in silent wrath. By the time he was finished, Adam and Eve looked as if they were wearing dark green scuba suits.

At least he was spared the sculpture of Lilith. A few years back the girlfriend of one of our benefactors decided to donate a sculpture of Lilith to our collection. Unfortunately for Efraim, the girlfriend was a renowned New York sculptor who argued it was ridiculous not to include the first woman created in the Garden of Eden in the exhibition. Efraim tried to fight it, explaining that it was more homiletical exegesis than biblical figure per se, but as usual, the big bucks tipped the scales.

I was standing next to Eli when the truck arrived and unloaded the New York Lilith, and together we watched Efraim lose his cool. She was naked, Lilith, tall, gigantic, hairy and stark naked. (Later the sculptor explained that she actually did try to be considerate and glue on her long dark hair so it would cover the more risqué bits, but the glue wore thin along the bumpy journey and revealed the sculptor's hyper-realistic styling of body parts.) And if that wasn't enough, she had her teeth sunk into a tiny baby. She looked like a predator.

I wasn't surprised, knew all the myths describing her as the enemy of mothers and devourer of babies, and even the sculptor explained, once the tumult died down, that her intent was merely to criticize the manner in which Lilith's character had been vilified: that she would never dream of eating her young, and that her only crime was her unwillingness to become the mother of a controlling man's children; but for Efraim it was a real lifesaver.

He knew that fighting liberal loons over exposed body parts was one battle he stood to lose, but over a woman devouring live babies? Come on.

Letters were sent, phone calls made and Lilith the cannibal was duly dispatched overseas to appear in the exhibition "The First Woman – The Last Mother," the sculpture's last known address.

But if you take a close look at the wax figurine of Eve, you can still see the crack that split open in her shoulder when she was moved in order to make room for Lilith, and got crushed against the wall. The shoulder area has since been restored, but the injury is still visible.

It's just how it is with Lilith, always leaving a trail.

My phone rings. I look at the name flashing on the screen and my heart skips a beat. *You idiot!*

I debate whether to answer right away or prolong the anticipation, then remind myself this isn't the usual tug of war we're playing here.

"Hey, Micha," I say, trying to find the right tone.

"Give me one good reason I shouldn't arrest you right now."

I freeze. From the corner of my eye, I notice little Miriam peeking from between the reeds.

"What… what are you talking about?"

"I'm talking about you bullshitting me about you and Dina not being in contact when it turns out you went over to her place the night she was murdered, that's what I'm talking about."

I feel the chill creeping through my entire body, *how does he know?* And that raw anger in his voice, with just a hint of violence. I was never good at dealing with direct accusations, always preferred the more indirect, roundabout way.

"I wanted to tell you," I drag the words out, "but I was afraid it wouldn't come off so well."

"It comes off like shit."

Okay, so definitely not the roundabout type. Little Miriam gazes at me with worry as I search for the right words, and keeps on gazing when they don't come. I hold the phone silently, a horrible, never ending, radiation-riddled silence. *Well, make something up already!*

"Look, Sheila," he says, and mentioning my name makes him sound a little friendlier. "What am I supposed to think? You didn't tell me the truth."

"Because I couldn't."

"Okay, so tell me now, slow and steady, why did you go to Dina Kaminer's?"

"She initiated it."

"Really?" he says, his tone once again devoid of sympathy. "Just like that? After twenty years?" He's asking the same questions Eli asked, but he's not Eli, *he's the opposite of Eli and you better keep that in mind.* "Or did you in fact keep in touch all this time? Maybe you lied to me about that too?"

"Look, I have to go teach a class, can we talk later?" I take a deep breath. "You can come over to my place, if you want." There, I said it. I feel the fear and foolishness jumbling in my stomach, like every time I make a destructive move. The wax figurine of Michal fixes her icy glare on me, the crown on her head sparkling.

"I'll come over, but this time no lies, Sheila, because I don't know where that will lead us." And he hangs up, leaving me clutching my phone, surrounded by wax figures whose gazes all say the same thing: *incorrigible.*

I walk into the instruction room, and Efraim immediately blurts out, "Well, hello there, good morning! Look who decided to show up! We were afraid some murderer had gotten to you as well."

Good morning to you too, Efraim. I know you mean well, or at least you think you do, but very soon I'll make you stop.

From across the room I exchange looks with my colleague Shirley, her consoling eyes telling me that she's already received her daily dose of "high risk single women" jokes.

Poor Efraim! If only he knew that Shirley was already making great strides towards getting pregnant via sperm donation, it would really have messed with his head, but eventually he'd reach the conclusion that it was a blessed event. Childbirth is always a blessed event. Obviously, if said baby came with a father, maybe even an observant father, it would make it all the more blessed, but Efraim has learned not to expect too much of his two spinsters – who also happen to be the best instructors on his team – so he's careful with his jokes. However, this particular murder seems to be beyond his self-restraint.

"Here are the reports Eli sent," I say, shoving them in his hands.

When Eli started working here, the mere mention of his name would bring a dreamy smile to Efraim's face, and he'd send me on all these ridiculous errands, fussing around me like a wrinkled old Cupid. Those good intentions again.

"Kill me now!" Yifat bursts into the room and collapses onto one of the chairs. "What an awful group, they wouldn't stop complaining the entire session."

"What do you expect from teachers?" the seasoned Efraim says. "Don't worry, it's all been taken care of; they just want a slight alteration in their lesson plan." He informs me that subsequent to recent events, this particular group of teachers from the settlement of Elkana in the West Bank is now interested in a "brief overview of that famous article by, you know, that friend of yours – but be gentle, Sheila, don't start up with all those aggressive opinions of yours."

That friend of yours. I once read that when someone uses that expression, more often than not they're referring to someone who isn't your friend at all. I take the instruction manuals and make my way to the auditorium, hearing from a distance the wax figurines bursting into giggles.

They're already waiting for me, sitting there chewing despite the No Eating sign hanging above the entrance to the auditorium.

A closed room crowded with religious women of child-bearing age has a very distinct smell, a combination of sweetness and acidity, the aroma of hormones, milk and blood. I feel the invisible babies nestled up against a few of them.

"Hello there," I begin. "I understand that, following recent events, you're interested in a brief review of Dina Kaminer's article." The words get stuck in my throat, but one should never show weakness, certainly not in front of a room full of teachers.

"Excuse me." It's one of them, the invisible baby clinging to her neck. "It's absolute hogwash. What does it even mean that women in the Bible didn't want to be mothers? Who doesn't want to be a mother?"

I look at her without blinking, taking in the smell of sweat and milk.

"Well, that theory certainly has quite a few detractors, but there were indeed several prominent biblical women who didn't have children, supposedly by choice. It might also explain the fact that many women in the Bible, including the nation's matriarchs, were portrayed as barren." I recite the essay's opening line, feeling my voice becoming lower, purring.

"What are you talking about?" a few of them exclaim in unison. "Those women begged for children, Rachel almost died childless!" I note to myself that Rachel eventually died in childbirth, but I don't want to incite the room, which is already starting to buzz with commotion.

"That's certainly the opinion of the biblical narrator," I reply calmly, "who was a man, of course, but he doesn't conceal the fact that some of the most active and accomplished women in the Bible, like Miriam the prophetess or Huldah the prophetess, didn't have children."

"A life without children is no life at all!" a woman shouts from the back of the auditorium. "Look at Michal, daughter of Saul, her punishment was a life without children."

"Punishment?" I reply. "Perhaps she simply wasn't interested in having children with the man who murdered her father and brother?" Michal's wax figurine flashes before me; maybe she's not sad at all, maybe her expression is one of relief, *I was spared.*

"Where did you come up with that nonsense?" Another one, ruddy and round, stands up in front of me, going on the warpath, *Don't take my motherhood away from me, it's all I have.*

"It's in the essay, dear," I reply peaceably.

"What essay? That's Kaminer's famous theory? That malarkey?"

"Call it whatever you like, but that theory gained her international acclaim, and has a very deep, serious factual basis."

"And how would you know?" It's the flushed one again, and she's standing so close to me now she almost looks cross-eyed; she's starting to resemble the wax figurine of our mother Leah, *melting babies to boot.*

"As a matter of fact, I was the one who helped Dina Kaminer develop the theory." Efraim, who happens to be passing by the auditorium on his way out, halts and fixes a curious gaze on me.

"Are you sure?" *Then how did you become such a loser?*

"Yes, I'm sure. Google it and see for yourself," I say, and hear the sound of all the wax figurines starting to applaud. With the exception of Miriam, of course, I can picture her evil eyes. A little girl standing between the reeds, frozen in time, never to grow up to be a leader, never to hold the drum.

By the end of the instruction class I revert back to my familiar calm and collected self again, including during the usual conciliatory closing round, in which each teacher likens herself to an inspirational biblical character. The ruddy one, as could be expected, chose Leah, the great matriarch. *Good for you, homegirl.* All that hormonal, milky sweat I have inhaled makes me a little sleepy and I almost blend into them to become one of them. As it was back then, living in the all-girls national service apartment, when after a while the little garbage can in the bathroom filled up with bloody sanitary pads on the exact same day, and later at the exact same hour. That subterranean female connection, working around the clock. *Tick-tock.*

And now, as I make my way home to prepare for Micha, I run through the list of suspects who could have told him about my meeting with Dina that evening, and none of the possibilities makes me very happy.

But only one makes me shudder at the mere thought.

6

HE'S COMING. *Tidy up the place, hide whatever needs to be hidden.* I rush through the rooms, checking every box, making sure that what happened last time won't happen again.

A quick sniff reveals the slightly dank odour coming from the plumbing system, *always the same smell.* I spray a few aggressive spurts of a special mist that's supposed to give my living room "the fresh floral aroma of spring," but unfortunately the whole apartment now reeks of a giant toilet. At least my sweaty clothes found their way to the bedroom; they've been sprawled out on the couch for over a week now, waiting to magically regain their former cleanliness and take on "the fresh floral aroma of spring."

I was never good at housekeeping. I remember the painfully brief period in which Maor and I lived under the same roof. I had a few reservations about it, a few fears, but they were probably misdirected, because what turned out to threaten my composure most (apart from having a very young and capricious partner) was the constant need to pretend I was adept at household chores. How often should the sheets be changed? When does the floor need mopping? What do you use to wipe the counter so it won't be rough and grimy? *What kind of mother will you be?* All those rags and dusters naturally placed by the sink in every home, what are they for? *What kind of mother will you be?* That mysterious business of "housekeeping."

A house doesn't need to be kept; oh, no, it's the one keeping you in its vice grip, chaining you to it by a string of clandestine tasks. "And that's when it's just the two of you," Shirley told me at the time, "just imagine what it's like when you have kids."

Believe me, I did.

A quick glance in the mirror, *Who are you trying to fool, Sheila? You're not waiting for a cop, you're waiting for a man.* I run my fingers through my hair, trying to fluff it up, and consider my face. *He's twenty-seven, and you have that new crease between your eyebrows.* Even if it is a fine, almost imperceptible line. It's true what they say about us women who've never given birth. We maintain our youthful look. Nature is on our side, aiding us in the deception, at least until we attract a suitable male, and then, only then, will we let our bodies collapse with a loud thud into gestation.

But nature also wants us to attract males of a suitable age, which is why the face wrinkles, someone once told me. The lines reflect the womb's biological state, so that young men can know what's happening inside you and you won't be able to fool them. I think it was Maor, he always liked presenting me with these fun bits of trivia. I even found it amusing at first.

I keep studying my face until a deafening knock on the door jolts me back into the present, and I realize that I forgot to hide the most important thing.

He barges in and stands in the middle of the living room; he's taller than I remembered, and his eyes much darker, a kind of dirty green, not to mention the expression.

Silent and hostile he stands before me, and I take a step back, praying he won't turn his gaze in the wrong direction. I try to enlist the help of polite gestures, imprinted on us by centuries of civilization, "Coffee?" My voice is warm and civil, "There's even milk." The image of Dina suddenly flashes before me, her small hands cradling the empty mug.

"Tell me, what were you doing there?" he asks in a churlish tone. "What were you doing at her house on the night of the murder?"

The night of the murder, the words sink deep inside me.

"I told you, she invited me over, we talked for a while, that's all."

"Oh, so it was a friendly conversation?" No. I don't like that tone one bit.

"Yes, pretty friendly, I think."

"You know what I think? That you're a shitty liar."

You're wrong, I'm an excellent liar.

"Pretty friendly," he parrots me mockingly. The impersonation, I must say, is surprisingly good. "Stop bullshitting me! She was scared to death of you, scared you'd kill her!"

"What?" I exclaim, hoping my shock sounds genuine. "Who told you such a thing?"

"Who do you think?"

I'll never say.

"Come on, Sheila." Even now, saying my name makes him sound a little more relaxed, but he's still standing firm in the middle of my living room, with those squinting green eyes, like a giant boa constrictor.

"Who even told you I was over there?"

"You tell me."

Not again with those silly cop-show games. "Has anyone ever, in your entire career, given you a straight answer to that 'you tell me'? Does that even work?"

He smiles despite himself, although it's definitely not the smile I was hoping for. *As the venom glands begin to swell, the snake appears to be smiling.*

"Ronit Akiva," he says, "she told me."

Thrump! Thrump! Of course it was her, and still it isn't easy for me to hear. Ronit's image flits before me, dark and beautiful, flashing that crimson smile of hers, *a man-eater.* That smile erases all other memories, apart from that final one.

"How does she look?" I can't believe that's the first thing to come out of my mouth.

"I have no idea, we spoke on the phone," he says, "but she's around your age, isn't she?"

Okay, I deserved that: ask a dumb question, get a dumb answer – and Ronit always did make me act like an idiot.

"It turns out your..." He pauses for a moment, "*friendly* chat with Dina scared her so badly that she called Ronit right after you left."

So the two were in closer contact than Dina was willing to admit, and this revelation makes me so angry I almost miss the implication of Micha's last few words.

"But that means when I left she was still alive!" I exclaim triumphantly. He pins me with a sharp gaze.

"It doesn't mean a thing. Maybe you went back there afterwards?"

My eyes bore into his, which have resumed their bright, soothing shade, and what I find inside them encourages me to continue: "Look at me, do you honestly believe I killed her? Come on, you actually think *I* tied her to a chair and glued a doll into her hands? How did they even manage with those tiny fingers of hers? Like a midget's hands." *Shut up, you moron.*

And once again his green gaze locks behind the thicket of eyelashes, casting about the apartment and lingering on the couch. He's searching for my doll, I know, but he won't find it, and the rest of the boxes are carefully sealed.

"I honestly don't know," he finally says. I guess that'll have to do for now.

When I bring him coffee, he's already sitting leisurely on the couch, one leg folded underneath his youthful body, full of bendable joints. I hand him the mug, and our fingers brush against each other.

"Did you add anything to this?"

"Other than sugar?" I consider him.

"You know what I mean."

Oh, yes, I definitely do. I felt it the moment he stepped into my house, the way he studied me, that something was certainly there. I never get these things wrong. I have no doubt the blame lies with Ronit, who opened her big painted mouth. "You tell me," I say. I just can't help myself, but he refuses to play along.

"Ronit said Dina was scared of you, afraid you cursed her or something."

Good.

"Then you can tell her from me to stop talking nonsense."

"She talked about it very seriously. Said that in college they called you the witch."

"Baloney," I reply, but suddenly, in what must have been the devil's work (or a witch's), the familiar song arises from the street, "Little witch, little witch fell down a ditch!" The small voices sound more menacing than usual, and despite my overwhelming urge to slam the window shut, I obviously won't do that in front of the suspicious green gaze.

"Are they singing about you?" he asks, feigning amusement, but it only makes him sound more serious.

"Of course not! What are you, crazy?"

"If that was your reputation in college, maybe you carried it into adulthood."

"Now you listen to me, it was a private joke between me and my friends, nothing serious, I just had... good instincts, intuition, that's all. Like how I knew the moment I saw you that you used to be religious."

"You don't need intuition for that, most religious people would have caught on to it within seconds."

"Or how I knew you were into more mature women."

He considers me carefully. "You don't have to be some gifted psychic for that either."

True, certainly not with all those looks and innuendoes of yours, which at present seem to have faded without leaving a trace. But I'm not worried: cute ex-Orthodox boys like you are invariably capricious, playing hot and cold with you, expecting you to be the supportive adult, until it blows up in both your faces, because you yourself happen to prefer being the little girl.

He picks up his mug, now cold. His eyes narrow as he studies the inscription, "To the Best Mum in the World."

And now he's tinkering with his teaspoon, eyeing it intensely, as if it will reveal to him everything he wants to know. I can't help but notice he hasn't taken even a tiny sip, just keeps on stirring.

"Have there even been any Jewish witches?" He's still stirring the coffee with those slow circular motions, like a witch over a bubbling cauldron.

"There were a few," I say, "but I promise you, I'm not one of them."

"Hypothetically," he says, stirring even slower now, "strictly hypothetically, what would you have slipped into my drink?"

I know I'm supposed to say now something like "a love potion," and I know that if I say it in a seductive, soft enough tone, I'd clear the air between us and maybe even more than that. But that slow stirring, the fact that he's barely looking at me, not to mention everything that happened with Ronit, who apparently stayed in touch with Dina after everything, *everything!*, that had gone down, all these result in me blurting out the word "poison," promptly followed by, "I'd slip poison in your drink."

He finally stops stirring, looks up at me and without blinking, draws the mug to his mouth and takes a big gulp. I stare at his Adam's apple. Yes, that was indeed a big, smooth swallow. Good boy.

"You know, we used to sing a different song when we were kids," he says. "Instead of 'Little Witch', we sang 'Old Spinster'. It went something like, *Fat old spinster, chin full of whiskers.*" He smiles at me while taking another sip of coffee, making me regret not lacing it with a deadly dose of poison.

7

My first encounter with Dina oddly resembled our last. Both took place in bright spaces, both involved women from the Bible and both certainly included a few "core essences imprinted in our DNA."

The first one took place during a Bible course in our freshman year at college. I vividly remember how I scrambled between the confusing auditoriums of Bar-Ilan University, lost, refusing to seek the assistance of the seniors who were stationed in the hallways for precisely that purpose. *Don't you dare show weakness.*

Eventually, I managed to find the right classroom, walking in beside the man who turned out to be our lecturer, a scrawny grey figure (grey from the hair on his head to his washed-out shirt and trousers). Passing him, I slightly brushed against him. He flinched, letting out a disapproving snort. Thinking back on it now, it might have been a snort of disgust, but to be sure, I would have had to see his expression.

Naama was already waiting for me in the back row, a few seats from Dina. I remember the bubblegum Dina was chewing with slow deliberation (cinnamon!), and the frighteningly intense way she stared at the lecturer.

Every time he used the expression "our sages of blessed memory," which he did quite often, she rolled her eyes (those dark, bulging eyes, cow eyes, but the smartest cow in the herd). The grey blob began with a quick overview of the biblical female characters he would be focusing on during the semester, and after he talked about Miriam ("the eldest sister"), Michal ("the king's daughter") and Leah ("the dutiful wife"), Dina leaned towards us (a faint whiff of cinnamon) and whispered, "Nothing good can come out of a man who views Miriam the prophetess as merely someone's 'sister.'"

The whisper echoed clearly through the auditorium, and the grey blob fell silent. His eyes cast about for the whisperer. Dina remained upright in her chair, unblinking, and I think that was the moment I realized I was sitting near to a fearless woman. Since I myself happened to be of the fear-riddled variety, I shrunk in my seat, and I think Naama did the same. The lecturer cleared his throat (I imagined it full of grey, cement-like phlegm), and said, "For your information, we will also be reviewing the character of Lilith, which our sages of blessed memory called – " and right then Ronit burst into the classroom, billowing black hair, mouth painted a fiery red, darting towards our row and collapsing into the last chair with a thud, just when the lecturer said, " – the unnamed woman, wicked, evil, whore."

"Jeez, thanks a lot," Ronit said in affront. Naama and I burst into laughter, while Dina tried to explain to her in loud whispers that he was talking about Lilith, who was actually an admirable figure. That was the straw that broke the blob's back, and eventually we were all kicked out of the classroom.

It was a warm, sun-stricken day, and we squinted at each other with slightly bashful smiles of early acquaintance, as we walked towards the bright grass mounds by the cafeteria. At this point of the story we were all alive.

"So back in college you were all close friends?" Once again that innocent tone belying more questions, none of them pleasant.

"The closest," I reply.

"How close?"

"I just told you, the closest."

"Lesbians?" While not a single muscle in his face moves, I almost fall off my armchair. *You don't want that, the floor's sticky and full of hairballs.* Obviously, I shouldn't be surprised; it always lingered in the air around Dina, a subtle but persistent aroma of whispers and rumours. At the bottom of every article about her, in the usual clump of comments, there were always some along the lines of "You disgusting lonely lesbian, you want to make everyone barren like you?" Once I almost informed one of them that most lesbians in fact do become mothers eventually, but it didn't feel like the right place to pursue that parley.

"Tell me, why is every strong woman immediately suspected of lesbianism?"

"Maybe it's just our way of coping."

He lowers his eyes with feigned humility, perfectly aware that he has just spewed out one the most inane psychologisms of all times, *our way of coping with it*, pfff! The atmosphere in the room shifts again, I just can't figure out in which direction.

"We were close friends in the traditional sense of the term," I say, trying to sound as frank as possible, "what you're talking about is mostly fantasies inspired by American college movies."

"Ulpana isn't that different," he says, with surprising insight into the world of the all-girls religious high school.

He's right. Girls are the same everywhere, the only difference being the abrupt change forced on you after years of being surrounded by only girls in the cushioning ulpana, when suddenly you're plummeted into college life where you're besieged with men. I remember what a struggle it was for me at first; I couldn't concentrate in class whenever a man happened to sit down next to me. Any male who innocently enquired where the Xerox machine was immediately found himself cast in the role of potential groom. Luckily, Dina and Ronit came along and saved me from all that. I mean, that's what I thought at the beginning.

"So why did that beautiful college friendship end?"

I wonder how much he knows exactly, reminding myself to proceed with caution, like a schoolgirl taking a test, knowing every point counts.

"I think you know," I say.

"You're right," he says, "that famous intuition at work." And he finishes his coffee, puts the mug down and asks in a rather friendly tone if I happen to have anything to eat.

Caught in the act. I have nothing to offer, neither a nosh nor a nibble. *What kind of mother will you be?* I open every kitchen cupboard, knowing perfectly well what I'll find there – that pile of awful candy from the corner store, half a box of stale cookies and a chocolate bar from the Elite kosher line for the ultra-Orthodox, which is barely a step above compound chocolate. A scene from *Mermaids* flashes before me – when Winona Ryder wants to make sandwiches for her object of infatuation, "a real sandwich, one that a man can sink his teeth into," and then her mother comes along (Cher, no less), and with the stroke of a cookie-cutter cuts them up into tacky little star-shaped sandwiches. Boom!

When I step back into the living room, I see he has moved a few things around the table, making room as if expecting a feast. I lower my gaze to the bowl in my hand, which contains two cookies and six squares of chocolate, suddenly noticing its lip is dirty. *What kind of mother will you be?*

"I understand you were a group of four," he says, and sinks his teeth into a piece of chocolate. "And then one of you passed away, and the beautiful friendship dissolved." He licks his lips when saying "passed away," and I think, what a pretty expression, "passed away," reserved, noble: "Naama passed away."

He takes another piece of chocolate, so old and stale you can barely see the symbol imprinted on it, shoves it into his mouth and starts sucking slowly, as if he has all the time in the world. We both know what he's waiting for.

"Naama committed suicide," I say. "Went and hanged herself."

"Sad story," he says, but doesn't sound the least bit sad; in fact, he sounds almost pleased.

A loud *bang* from the bedroom makes us jump up; it sounds like a gunshot. Micha sprints towards the bedroom door, not before shooting me a suspicious look. I rush after him, the only thought on my mind is that the room is a desperate, unventilated mess.

We both fix our eyes on the fallen shelf, and on the nearly empty water glass that is now shards on the floor. *Don't walk in barefoot, Sheila.* I stare with horror at the several pairs of pants strewn about; a single frayed bra, yellowing with age, is gaping before him, covered entirely in bits of glass, as if inlaid with precious gemstones. *Precious and rancid.*

"How did this happen?" he asks.

"I'd like to know that myself," I reply, recalling a similar instance in my old apartment. I had just moved in with Maor when the shelf collapsed with a loud thud in the middle of the night; I woke up screaming. Maybe these shelves are equipped with sensors alerting you to dubious young men.

"Looks like the suspension mechanism is shoddy," he says, while examining the shelf up close, his words lingering in the air. Neither of us brings up Naama again, but she's hanging between us, with the rope she tied around her neck, *black, they said.*

I study him as he fixes the shelf back onto the wall. There's something confidence-instilling in a man labouring for you with his hands; in his case, large, squarish hands, while his movements are gentle, almost feminine, but there's nothing feminine about a man putting up shelves. He gathers up the bits of glass while I stand by the door, staring at him like an idiot.

"Say, what did Dina look like?" I can't help myself.

"You were her friend," he replies without meeting my eye.

"You know what I mean."

"Yes, well, I was hoping I was wrong," he says drily. That doesn't stop me.

"I have to know, when they carved the word 'mother' into her forehead, was there a lot of blood?" I picture Dina, her big dark eyes gazing blindly ahead, streams of blood trickling down from the open wound. *Becoming a mother always hurts.*

"You're crazy."

"So, was there a lot of bleeding?"

"Not even a little, actually," he replies, still not looking at me.

"Huh. That means they carved it post-mortem," I say, enlisting one of my many facts acquired through binge-watching hospital shows. "I guess that's something."

But why on her forehead, why? The area reserved for the mark of Cain; since when is motherhood a curse? Motherhood has always been synonymous with valour and virtue, hasn't it? At least in this neck of the woods. And all this time I'm creeping up behind him, until finally I'm close enough to kick the stinky yellowing bra under the bed and make it disappear.

Unfortunately, that's exactly the moment he decides to turn around.

"What are you doing?"

"Nothing."

"What are you trying to hide there?" And he reaches out and yanks the bra out from under the bed. It stretches, and when he lets go, splinters of glass ricochet onto his hand, grazing his fingers. We both gape at the fine droplets of blood. He takes the filthy bra, shakes it and wraps it around his hand, God help me.

"The reason Dina didn't bleed is because they didn't carve the word 'mother' on her forehead, they just wrote it," he says quietly.

"Wrote?" I ask, still focused on his hand swathed in my bra like a stuffed cabbage roll. "You mean with a pen?"

"No."

"Marker?"

"No."

"Bodily discharge?"

"Don't be a pervert."

You ain't seen nothing yet, my friend, I think to myself and say, "I'm the pervert? What about the person who did that to her?"

He remains silent.

"Paintbrush?"

"No."

"Chalk? Eyeliner?"

"Getting warmer," he replies.

"So it has to do with make-up?"

"Hot, hot, boiling," he says in a tone that brings to mind the child he once was, which, I remind myself, wasn't that long ago.

"Maybe lipstick?" I ask.

"Good job, Detective," he says. "They wrote it in lipstick."

I'm still processing that "detective," when it dawns on me that there's only one colour possible. "Did it happen to be red lipstick?"

"You're getting better at this," he says, waving his bandaged hand. "Blood-red."

I close my eyes. "Interesting," I remark, "Dina was against using lipstick, using any make-up really."

Like everything else with Dina, this too was a matter of principle. She had no qualms about buying the finest, most expensive clothes, or grooming that lush dark hair of hers, but she was adamantly against any kind of make-up. *Don't paint on masks, my sisters*, but she never had to trick young men about her reproductive viability, did she? She never had to hide her fading youth with layers of make-up. *What you see is what you get.*

"We're certainly aware of all that," he says, "and we have a few interesting leads." Almost despite himself, his gaze is drawn to my make-up set, particularly to my collection of lipsticks standing to attention like a row of soldiers. I spare him the need to ask.

"Blood-red isn't my colour, Mister Police Officer." I smile at him and almost – just almost – spew out the rest of the sentence, "but I happen to know whose colour it is."

8

JUST LIKE BACK THEN, in college, all eyes are on Ronit. Some linger by our table, trying to figure out where they recognize her from, and there's a weirdo standing at a distance, taking a photo on his mobile phone. At least he's not coming over to our table to ask for a selfie.

Obviously, she's enjoying every moment of this, Ronit, despite her feeble attempts to pretend she isn't. She was never good at pretending, *never really tried, which is exactly why you hated her.* I feel the familiar acid crawling up my oesophagus and quickly bury my face in the menu, only then noticing that it's the child's menu. SpongeBob SquarePants is blowing me a puckered kiss.

Ronit smiles at me with those lush lips of hers, painted with the same old red lipstick down to the garish sub-tone. With those giant, bee-stung lips she could afford that blood-red. I, with my thin lips, stay a mile away from dark shades. They make my mouth look like a shrivelled and shrunken raisin.

"He's really cute, that Micha, isn't he?" she asks and flashes me a smile, which I do not return.

That liar showed his cards that very evening.

He stepped out of my bedroom, carrying his bandaged hand like a wounded soldier. On his way to the living room, he paused in the hallway and stared straight ahead. My heart sank. I knew he wouldn't miss the painting, the one I'd foolishly forgotten to take down before he arrived.

"*The Witch of Endor*," he read the cursive script at the bottom, and his face turned sombre. I doubt any man would be happy with this painting. The Witch of Endor is depicted there at the peak of her power, mid-air, her wavy hair flowing in the wind, with an almost obscenely giant broomstick sticking out from between her legs.

"Looks a lot like the painting hanging at Dina's house," he said, eyes still fixed on the broomstick. "Same painter?"

"Not at all. And they look nothing alike," I replied. We both knew I was lying.

"And doesn't the woman in the painting look a little like your friend Ronit?"

"Ronit? She might have looked like that years ago." Any mention of Ronit's name ruffled my feathers, not to mention that I didn't appreciate the comparison. Not one bit.

"I'm talking about how she looked two days ago, when I saw her."

"But you told me you didn't see her. You lied to me!"

He just stood there, wearing his smug grin. But he didn't surprise me, not really. Deep down I knew he met with her, knew it from the way he talked about her, the way his eyes shone.

Like Lilith before her, Ronit always left a trail.

And now she's sitting in front of me, languidly flipping through a magazine, her smile stretching wider with every page she turns. Her teeth are perfectly aligned, giant pearls, as if they were lasered and polished an hour ago. Obviously, her image is splayed across the magazine's glossy cover under the declaratory headline, "I was Dina Kaminer's best friend."

The deranged photographer decided to photograph her holding a baby doll, and the equally deranged editor chose that photo for the cover. She was sitting on a chair, dressed as a Madonna, her face beaming at the doll in her hands. *At least they didn't have to glue it there.* As if shedding her signature seductiveness, her expression is soft and wistful, her eyes radiating fake maternal tenderness. She reminds me of someone, but I just can't remember who.

If I was wondering what kind of relationship she and Dina maintained after college, the article provided me with the delightful answer: a tenuous one, if any. The journalist's sycophantic questions were met with anecdotes and vignettes from our time on campus, including one about our graduation party, *not including that particular fancy dress party*, and the obvious clichés about "kindred spirits" and "sisters in the struggle." She looks at her own photos transfixed, holding the magazine closer and further away from her beguiled gaze, as if she would chew and swallow it whole if she could.

I feel like telling her that not once in her entire lagging career as an actress had she been awarded a cover, and that she had to wait for her "best friend" to be murdered to finally get one. But I remind myself that lurking behind the dark red lipstick are those giant teeth of hers, just waiting to bite.

Like Dina, Ronit has barely changed, providing further proof that women without children get to keep their youthful appearance. *Stop hunting for evidence, it's a fact and that's that.* The black, unruly shock of hair is still here, in all its former glory, towering above the same thick eyebrows and the deep dimple in her chin. She looks smoother somehow, as if her body has been vigorously plucked. But other than that, it's the same body, slender and toned, with those same liberated and sensual movements that make whoever's sitting in front of her cringingly aware of their own body.

I remember I used to think her extravagant sexuality compensated for some deficiency, maybe even arctic frigidness, but unfortunately, I was proved wrong. Naama was the one who taught me there were no surprises in that area, "Our mind-numbing lecturer won't suddenly turn out to be an animal in bed, and you won't catch Meira the librarian at a swingers party. What you see is what you get, and someone who oozes sexuality oozes it for a reason." Noticing my disappointed expression, she added, "It's okay, I'm not a big fan of Ronit's theatrics either. She'll probably grow out of it in a few years."

It's a shame I can't tell her that despite the considerable passing of time, she hasn't grown out of it. As proof, she's now sticking her finger in the little bowl of honey and licking it, her tongue the same vermilion as her lips.

She leans closer to me, and I pick up a funny, sweet smell. Gone is the subtle lemony scent of her Blue Lagoon, the perfume she wouldn't let any of us buy because it was "hers." Whatever the brand, her new smell is exotic aggression. And maybe every age exudes its own special smell, and what we thought was the scent of her Blue Lagoon, was just the intoxicating fragrance of youth itself.

A few years ago, one of the Israeli late-night TV shows hosted Eighties' icon Samantha Fox. She looked fabulous (childless, what else), and the thrilled host told his next guest, who had been blindfolded, that he had to guess the person sitting beside him. I remember the guest being led to the couch where Samantha was sitting. He took one sniff of her neck and promptly announced: "Well, young she ain't."

The fortyish-year-old Samantha gave her polite British smile, and the visibly embarrassed Israeli host refused to translate the guest's remark for her. I remember wondering what it was about her smell that made him reach his swift conclusion. And now, taking in Ronit's new smell, I realize it reveals something deep and internal, something inside the bloodstream. It turns out the body has its own bag of tricks to betray its age, no matter how hard you try to hide it.

A young woman bursting with shopping bags approaches our table and stutters, "Is that you, on the magazine? I wasn't sure." She looks surprised and excited, and Ronit smiles, as proud as a puffed-up peacock. Doesn't even bother hiding it.

"Good for you, really," she tells Ronit. "Not every woman has to have kids, I'm a big supporter of your cause. And hats off for the essays, super important."

Ronit is still smiling, but her tone is cautious, "Thanks, sister, but it's important to remember that Dina Kaminer was the driving force and the woman who, hmm… wrote the essays."

I stare at her with leery distrust. Modesty has never been her strong suit.

"And if you're interested in the subject, you can talk to Sheila over here," she continues. "She's actually the one who gave Dina the idea for that groundbreaking essay."

Something's definitely wrong. Ronit doling out credit? Ronit paying me a compliment? *Publicly??*

"Oh, you're into that too?" the young woman enquires in a friendly tone. "So, none of you want kids? What is this, the national childfree women's conference?" she asks, then gives us a polite, light-hearted giggle and walks away, but doesn't forget to turn around, raise her hand and part her index and middle fingers in a cheerful V-sign. *One day we'll rule the world. And render humanity extinct.*

Ronit and I don't dare look at each other.

"Say, why did you tell that detective that I'm a suspect?" The silence congeals into a sticky goo, and it feels like the right moment to get down to business. "You honestly think I killed Dina?" *If I didn't kill her sixteen years ago, you think I'd do it now?*

She takes her time answering, still fishing the pine nuts out of the ginormous salad she ordered, still sipping her coffee without leaving lipstick traces on the mug, just like she never left any traces on the styrofoam cups back in college. *Her traces are of an entirely different variety.*

"That detective," she parrots me, "who do you think you're fooling? His name is Micha and you obviously have a crush on him."

Ronit might be an actress, but as a mimic, she can't hold a candle to him. Not that I have any intention of sharing that information with her.

"I see your man-picker is still off," she says. "Same old same old."

A tall figure flashes before my eyes. Neria. My first *and certainly not last* mistake. But at twenty you're allowed to make mistakes. The only problem is that my twenties are so far behind they're a dot in my rear-view mirror, and I'm still making a twenty-year-old's mistakes.

"So did you or did you not tell him I'm a suspect? That Dina was afraid of me?"

"Look, I remembered how much you love being the centre of attention, so I did you a favour," she giggles. "It worked, didn't it?" she asks, and her giant, scarlet pie hole opens wide with laughter.

No, she isn't mourning Dina's death either. I consider her, this laughing, frivolous Ronit, this *wicked, evil, whore* with her mammoth mouth agape just like it was back then, that night, *We're just messing with you, jeez, you're so uptight,* with that same gaudy lipstick like a bloody stain. With the raised knife, and the scream, so full of anguish, with Ronit doubled over in laughter. *Thrump! Thrump! Thrump!*

"I'm messing with you, Sheila, it's just a joke, jeez," she says, "where's your sense of humour?"

"I never did care for your dumb jokes," I hiss. "You're confusing me with Naama. She was the only one who liked them."

That shuts her up. Nothing like dredging up a corpse to make someone clam up. Especially when the head count is now two dead and two living. Ronit sticks her fingers back in her salad and starts tweezing out pine nuts again, and I wonder whether she ever talked about Naama over the years. When she met with Dina, her "best friend," did she allow herself to share certain memories, or did they both just put her behind them, leave her there swaying on her rope, forgotten?

"Did Dina even talk about her?" I can't help myself.

"What do you think? Of course not!" There it is, the faint but familiar note of aggression. "And I already told you, it's not like Dina and I were close!"

"Didn't keep you from giving that interview," I say.

"I always said, if life gives you lemons, make lemonade," she says calmly. I can't believe she actually used that stale cliché, but then again, Ronit was never the sharpest lemon on the tree.

"Besides, I'm about to star in a TV show about four friends, so the interview came just in time. I don't think Dina would have minded."

At least she's not giving me the whole "that's what Dina would have wanted" spiel, because we both know nothing could be further from the truth. *You don't get to piggyback off my fame.*

"And there's a song there that really reminded me of us," she says and pauses for a second, "I mean, our old us. It goes like this:

"Four little girls, playing with their dollies,
Snap! went one – and then there were three.
Three little girls, playing with their dollies,
Off came a head – as broken as could be.
Two little dollies, one disappeared,
And then there was one – just as she'd feared."

Her singing voice is a creaky, low-pitched whine.

"Sounds like a children's song," I say, despite the fierce urge to get up and run far, far away.

"I don't like children's songs," she replies.

"No one does."

"And no one likes children," she says, and we both belt out the rest, "and no one wants kids, and no one needs kids, and we'll never ever have them, n-e-v-e-r!"

Our voices, crooning off-key, are the voices of twenty-year-old students.

*

I want to go home, now. Never mind that I didn't get what I wanted out of Ronit, I just want to get out of here.

I start mumbling the "We should probably get the check" routine, but she, instead of jumping at the opportunity to bolt and make sure she never has to bump into me again, says, "Let's order another coffee."

Is it just my imagination or have the mugs on the table turned into the styrofoam cups from the campus coffee machine? *It is your imagination. Now pull yourself together and get what you want out of her.*

"So what about this Micha?" she says casually, as if we're picking up a conversation where we had left off years ago, on the grass by the campus cafeteria. "He's just your type."

There's something disturbing about the fact that we haven't seen each other in sixteen years and she can still nail my taste in men.

"Maybe I actually did do you a favour," she says with her smug smile. "I'm guessing he called you with more questions about Dina, and maybe you even met again? You remember I always liked playing matchmaker."

She stretches out in her chair and the top button of her blouse opens, revealing the curvature of her breasts, which, like the rest of her, are perfectly preserved. Two firm apples. *Nothing like your shrivelled pears that look like they nursed triplets.*

"Don't bullshit me," I say, "the last thing you care about is helping me."

"You always were ungrateful," she replies, straightening her blouse but leaving the top button open. "You should be thanking me."

"For what exactly?"

"Maybe for not telling him everything I know?"

Button up your goddamn blouse. "What could you have told him?"

"What you did to me back then."

"Back then?" There's only one "back then" she can be talking about. "What did I do to you? I did something to you?"

"You most certainly did," she says and pauses in expectation. "Oh, please, don't pretend you don't remember, you broke my hand."

That night. I look down at her hands. *Thrump! Thrump!* Dina was the one drumming, Ronit just stood there laughing her head off, even when she heard that *agonized* scream, even when... I keep staring at her hands, strong and steady, *hands that can apply lipstick perfectly, without going outside the lines.*

"Sheila, don't give me that 'who, me?' face. You knocked me backwards and broke my hand."

"I only nudged you!"

"You pushed me, violently, on purpose. I broke a bone. Don't tell me you don't remember."

"I remember no such thing."

She narrows her eyes at me, the look reflected in them decidedly unpleasant, as is her voice when it emerges from her ruby lips that suddenly seem paler, "Well, if that's the case, I have to wonder what else you conveniently forgot."

9

I HAPPEN TO HAVE a strikingly good memory, Miss Ronit. As striking as your smudge-proof lipstick, which, as if by magic, leaves not a single mark on your coffee cup.

And now, as if to taunt me, you're biting into the Danish you ordered along with your weak Americano. Tell me, where does it all go? I put my hand on the roll of flab spilling over my waistband, nature's idea of a birthday gift to most women hitting forty, whether they've cranked out a baby or not. Maor actually liked my muffin top, or at least that's what he said when pinching it. But Maor liked saying a lot of things that weren't necessarily true. *I'm telling you, I have absolutely no interest in becoming a father.*

So, my strikingly good memory, Miss Ronit, might not be the killer memory I had twenty years ago (turns out you don't need the whole post-partum brain fog for that, your memory will eventually start going downhill with age; probably too many memories better left forgotten), but you won't make me doubt what happened or didn't happen, what broke or didn't break that night. I'm not some heroine in a book who finds out halfway into the plot that she has actually murdered her entire family with an axe and repressed the heinous memory. Oh, come on, Miss Ronit, that won't be my story.

"So why didn't they rape her?" Ronit's voice may be soft but the note of ruthlessness is definitely there, rearing its ugly head. *That old ruthlessness.*

"Because it wasn't about that, it was about motherhood," I reply very slowly.

"Yes, but they were going to kill her anyway, right? And whoever did it has to be a complete perv, so why not rape her as well?"

"Maybe he didn't want to shift the focus from his statement?" I hang my gaze on my empty plate while Ronit continues to chew her Danish. And maybe gluing a doll to someone's hand *and* marking her forehead *and* working up the passion is just too complicated? *"Rape Is Not an Expression of Passion, Rape Is an Expression of Violence and Control," a lecture by Dr Dina Kaminer, 2nd semester.*

But I have to say I thought about it myself.

"Or maybe they did rape her and they're just not telling us?" Ronit smacks her blood-red lips as if she's just thought of something delicious. It was a swift gesture, as quick as a bullet, but I saw it. "That Micha is hiding something, you listen to me."

"Even if he is hiding something," *and he is*, "I don't think it's rape. It just doesn't add up. They turned her into a mother, a Madonna, a saint."

"Well then, classic Madonna–whore complex."

"Ronit, I'm telling you, that isn't the case here; this isn't Eve and Lilith." That shuts her up real fast. "Whoever did this knew perfectly well what he wanted to accomplish, and I don't think rape was one of the objectives." Or not the only one. To be Dina's friend was to run the whole gamut of ugly emotions: frustration, jealousy, resentment, to name a few.

"Fine. Between you and me, I don't think he would have had much fun anyway." She bites into her Danish and a tiny glob of jam smears her chin. She doesn't wipe it.

"What do you mean?"

"She was never a very sexual person."

"What are you talking about? Her sexuality has nothing to do with rape."

"Don't play dumb. The woman's already dead, you can stop being afraid of her. She was practically asexual."

Sex is *power*, and Dina had power, that much is obvious, but where did it come from? I think back on the long, sultry days of summer, when we sprawled on the beach. Dina looked like a giant cat, napping in the sun, *but she always kept one eye open. What was it fixed on, that open eye?*

"You remember that Purim party, when her brother put his hand on you?"

How could I forget that party? It's where it all started, *and it still hasn't ended.*

"What about it?"

"Dina didn't like it. Think why."

I look at Ronit as she leans closer with wolfish eye and says, "Think hard."

I am thinking hard, but not in the direction Ronit's hinting at. Young Dina always took an interest in whoever grabbed her shy brother's attention. But Ronit can't be implying that Dina was actually… can she?

"God, no!" she cries out, as if reading my mind. "Way off base. You're gross."

I'm the gross one?

"She was a control freak, and when sex comes into the picture, a lot of times things get out of control." She finally finishes her sticky Danish and licks her oily red lips. "That's what bothered our Dina, and I'm asking myself whether this has something to do with what bothered our killer."

Oh, now it's *our* killer. Very interesting.

"What do you make of him writing on her forehead with red lipstick?"

I stare at her lips, still shimmering with butter, as if she has just devoured a small animal.

"Come on," she laughs and dabs her glistening lips with a napkin, as if leaving an oily kiss for a secret admirer. "You're not trying to imply it was me, are you?"

"At least I'm not setting detectives on you," I say. *Nope, I'm keeping them all for myself.*

"You can set as many as you like," she replies with a smile. "At least that means you're no longer afraid of me stealing your men." And once again Neria's lanky image flits before me, *fair curls, brown eyes*, and the young Ronit who wasn't allowed anywhere near him, the Ronit who, only a few weeks into our freshman year, earned herself the reputation of *man-eater.*

"I'd watch it if I were you," I say.

"But you're not me," she retorts with a grin, "although you'd like to be."

A young Orthodox couple sits down at a nearby table. I quickly tug my skirt over my knees but then remember that I'm in the more liberal Ramat Gan, and I hike it back up and spread my legs open just a little bit wider. The baby in their stroller won't stop squealing, but they just keep their indifferent eyes on their menus. I wonder what kind of kid he'll grow up to be with all that attention.

Yesterday, while ambling down a side street in Bnei Brak, I walked past two kids sitting on the kerb, one of them mind-blowingly fat. The street was empty and the whale of a kid mumbled in my direction, "kurve." A whore? Nice. It wasn't the flattering kind of kurve, but an automatic kurve without so much as a trace of lewdness. I turned around and ripped into him, "You're a kurve!" He was terror-stricken, as if he couldn't believe I would answer him. It's highly possible that if the street hadn't been empty, I would have swallowed the insult and kept walking. And you can bet none of the passers-by would have told him off. The only thing that mattered to them was that the street loudspeakers came on at the right time to announce the arrival of Shabbat and blare its tune: "Privilege me to raise children and grandchildren." Who knows, maybe one of those children will grow up to be as lovely a creature as the foul-mouthed blob-fish on the kerb.

I keep my eyes on the couple at the adjacent table. She's one of those prim and manicured Orthodox frummies, the kind who keeps her willowy figure even after a thousand births (and there will be just about a thousand), but the husband is just a bespectacled putz. Ronit is eyeing me eyeing them.

"Why did you move back to Bnei Brak anyway?" she asks.

"Because I don't have to pay rent there," I reply, "and besides, it's not Bnei Brak, it's on the border."

Ronit snickers blood-red.

"Don't try to sell me that one," she says. "My apartment is on the border of Ramat Gan. You live in Bnei Brak, honey."

The baby is still shrieking, and his parents are still ignoring him. Ronit stares at the baby with a pensive gaze. "Do you know the human ear can't bear a baby's scream? It's literally ear-splitting. Nature created us that way."

I recall the squeals of other babies, and the soothing words that always followed, *Little baby... sweet little munchkin... don't cry...* It seems like Ronit reads my mind because she suddenly shoots up and walks out of the café, far from the squeals the human ear can't bear, especially not her human ear.

When Ronit's back, her face is beaming with the idiotic smile of a twenty-year-old student.

"Look who I found outside," she says, holding the door for a tiny, scrawny woman pushing a double stroller carrying twins.

The vicious delight in Ronit's voice makes me cast a glance at the woman. Then a second glance, followed by a third. Tali Unger. Taliunger. Of course. Only she could make Ronit sound so very pleased.

"Sheila! How are you? It's been years!" As always, Taliunger's feigned geniality is so intense that an innocent bystander might be fooled into believing she's actually happy to see me.

I remember her well from college. Even then she was as thin as a steel wire, with woolly hair and that awful skin permanently caked with what looked like buttercream frosting. She was the lead organizer of the various student protests on campus, and we used to laugh at her, saying that it was the only way she could interact with boys. I remember watching her sprawled on the floor, colouring the giant sign they later hung across the university bridge: "Don't Give Them Guns!" Colouring in the outline of a rifle, her hand was just a few inches away from Boaz's, the hottie from the student union who was colouring the background. She kept moving her hand closer to his until the backs of their hands almost touched. When she noticed me staring, I smiled, and she quickly pulled her hand away. It wasn't just me, she loathed all of us, the whole group.

And there was that Purim party, when she dressed up as a baby, with a giant pacifier plugging her mouth and a white baby bonnet on her scouring-pad hair. It seemed like she had chosen that costume just to provoke us, but she looked so pathetic and wretched that I almost felt sorry for her (and it wasn't entirely her fault, back then costume catalogues didn't offer a *sexy baby* ensemble). We, on the other hand, dazzled in carefully selected, artfully chosen get-ups. Dina, tall and striking in her wavy cape, approached her, plucked the pacifier from her mouth and, ignoring the thread of shining spittle stretching from the dummy, kissed her right on her lips.

"Happy Purim, baby," she purred and winked at her. "You're such a cute little baby I almost want to adopt you." And another kiss, this time on her cheek, after which Dina turned and walked away with the three of us trailing behind her, capes billowing. Taliunger stood frozen to her spot in the middle of the auditorium, stupefied, eyes darting in panic, a filament of spit dangling from her lower lip. The hateful glares would come later.

So why is Ronit looking at her now with such affection?

"Did you know that Tali is married to Neria Grossman?"

Well then.

There's nothing but care and concern in Ronit's voice, but her eyes tell a whole other story. *Remind her that you broke up with Neria and not the other way around, go on, remind them both!* But on the all-female playground, Taliunger won a crucial match, and this fact is lost on no one.

"Tali and I are neighbours," Ronit goes on, "but actually, if you moved back to Bnei Brak, that means we're all neighbours."

Taliunger (I should start getting used to Taligrossman, since there's next to zero chance she kept her maiden name) looks at me, opens her little mouth to say something but changes her mind and snaps it back shut. In lieu of words she offers a few fake coughs, *the kind that hide a nasty remark.*

"Maybe the three of us can be a group," she finally says, curtly. Ronit and I exchange glances.

"You never got married, did you?" Tali asks me in a statement posing as a question, her little mouth a crack in the thick stratum of make-up.

"Nope," I reply casually.

"And what about kids?" That's an outright challenge, and we both know it.

"What do you think?" I ask her. *Tick-tock, tick-tock.*

"No," she replies, "I'm guessing no kids."

"Well, your impressive crop is enough for both of us."

"Mine and Neria's," she corrects me in a sickly sweet tone, and I feel like congratulating her for lasting as long as she did without mentioning him. Just as she utters his name, one of her twins bursts into such deafening, blood-curdling cries that we freeze into stillness. Twin one's wailing naturally triggers twin two's howls, and as if to prove he can hold his own, the Haredi baby at the nearby table, who had calmed down in the meantime, joins the horrendous cryfest. The cacophony soon melds into one shrill, scathing scream, as if the three babies have formed an amateur a cappella ensemble.

Tali leans over the stroller to soothe the twins, and her soft maternal touch and comforting words stir inside me the memory of little hands reaching out for me, a voice calling out from the darkness, *Munchkin! Itty-bitty baby! Who wants a cuddle? No, I'll drop her. No, you won't, don't be an idiot, who wants a cuddle, who? And that smile, I'll drop her. No, Dina, you won't drop her, how could you? They glued her to your hands.*

10

"YOU WANT WHAT?" Eli's hamster eyes narrow before me. I reach for the Coke can on his desk, resting atop a towering pile of papers, but he stops me. *Not today, Missy.*

By the way he just put his hand between me and his Coke, I realize this is going to be even harder than I thought. Ever since we talked about "the detective," as Eli refers to him, he's no longer my easy-going, easily manipulated friend.

"I want you to come to Ronit's birthday party with me," I repeat, nice and slow, and add, "It's tonight. Tali Unger is coming too."

It's always best to give out all the information at once. Or at least, most of the information. And Eli has heard enough from me about Miss Unger.

"Explain it to me. Why exactly do you want to go to that party?"

Take a wild guess.

"Because I think Ronit is involved somehow, or she at least knows more about the murder than she's letting on. I didn't care for that *chance encounter* with Tali Unger, not one bit."

And that's certainly the truth. Not that I wanted to go, but watching Tali squirm when Ronit invited me to her party, I just had to say yes. A thousand times yes. *You can't have it all, Miss Taliunger.*

"Oh, yes, Tali Unger. The woman who prevailed where you failed," Eli quips, feigning a light-hearted laugh, but we both know it's true. I pick up the Coke can and take a sip, pumping free radicals straight into my bloodstream. He doesn't stop me.

"Why don't you be honest with yourself and just admit you feel like brushing up against the past, and maybe see Neria Grossman again?"

My grip tightens on the can, but it doesn't crush as nicely as it does in the movies.

A sharp angle grazes my pinkie finger, producing a long thin scratch, just like the one I got after my last meeting with Neria; *the last chance encounter, not the last awful planned one.* Images from that encounter flash before me – Neria sitting on a street bench, vigorous and robust as ever, me happening to pass by after a long and ugly bout of mono, dragging my feeble body down the street. What can I say? Fate and its famous humour. We both uttered the perfunctory "Oh, hello there," and "It's been years!" and "So how have you been?" but he felt the need to add, "You know, I hardly recognized you." I, on the other hand, instantly recognized him, especially the nasty edge that crept into his voice. But I felt l had it coming after what I did to him, *after what Dina did to him.*

So I smiled and kept my mouth shut, but on the way home I stopped at a drugstore and bought ten different kinds of vitamins and minerals to boost hair, skin and nail health, and when I got home, I opened all the small bottles and tore into the pill sheets, scraping my finger on the vitamin B-complex wrapper. Which is when I finally burst into tears. *Little witch, little witch fell down a ditch, scraped her finger and broke into whimpers.*

"Trust me, I'm in no hurry to see Neria again," I say.

"Then why do you want me to go to the party with you?"

Why do you think.

"Because you're a fastidious accountant, that's why; you notice every detail, and people who know Ronit and maybe Dina are going to be there. We might find out new information."

He takes the crinkly can from me, peers inside to make sure it's empty and tosses it into the garbage can, *a good accountant never wastes a thing.* "Sheila, it has nothing to do with the murder. You just want a man by your side there, that's all. Don't be embarrassed."

But I am embarrassed, Eli, you little hamster, and anyway, when did we start telling each other the whole truth and nothing but? What's so nice about friendships is that friends don't have to share everything with each other, certainly not the truth, which is usually ugly and insulting. So yes, given that I'm likely to run into a few figures from my decidedly unglamorous past there, I'd indeed prefer to have a man by my side, especially a submissive, docile one like you, who'd let me ignore him the entire night. How's that for the truth, huh, Eli?

He must have noticed a slight change in my expression, because he immediately says, "Don't worry, I'll go with you." To which I reply, "Thanks, you're the only person I trust," and while my mouth is chewing out the words, I realize it's the truth.

Then he just has to ask, "You haven't heard anything from that detective?"

That detective. I see we aren't quite ready to call him Micha yet. And no, I haven't heard anything new, and I have no idea whether that's a good or bad sign. *It's an excellent sign, you stupid baby.* I automatically reach for my phone, and no, no missed calls. *And how could there be any, when you've been staring at the damn thing all day?*

The press also took half a step back, I mean the news pages, because the magazines were still brimming with the shock waves; just this Saturday, one of the women's magazines featured a piece about "religious couples who choose not to have children," or at least that's what the tantalizing title advertised, but the reporter did everything within her power to wrest a limp promise out of each of the miserable couples that maybe, down the road, they'd reconsider their choice, that "maybe one day..." In a predictable yet ludicrous manner, the reporter pointed the finger of blame solely at the wives, while the husbands were granted full immunity and sympathizing support. One of them bore a remarkable resemblance to Eli.

"It'll be okay, don't worry," he says, and it takes me a few seconds to realize he's talking about Ronit's party. He's completely clueless about what he has agreed to because he doesn't know Ronit, but I have no doubt that's about to change. He'll get to know her all right. The moment we step into her party together, she'll be all over him. A scorpion never changes, *and neither does a Lilith.* I stick my pinkie in my mouth and taste the warm, soothing blood.

It's the night of the survivors.

I look up at Ronit's bright balcony, hear the voices carried in the air, *whispers and giggles.* I feel Eli's body tense beside me. He looks exactly the way I wanted him to: a solid partner, but the kind of partner no one can quite figure out. *There comes a time in every woman's life when obfuscation is her best companion.* Just as I start sucking in my stomach, I remember I don't have to. I have my organ-crushing Lycra shapewear on for that. Sure, I'm sweating from every pore under this cling-film bodysuit, but like the saleswoman said: A building's most important feature is its foundation, and yours could use a little reinforcement. *And the most important parts of the foundation are the ones you can't see.*

The moment we step into the spacious, well-lit apartment, I'm instantly struck by the smell of alcohol, sweat and expensive perfumes. *Eau de cougar.* I take in IKEA's version of a living room, complete with several nondescript landscapes on the walls. *Well, well, turns out the seductive siren has the soul of a coupon-clipper.* She even has the bulky EKTORP in off-white, possibly the ugliest armchair ever made. Currently sitting on this eyesore is a woman I vaguely recognize as an actress who starred in a commercial for some feminine hygiene product, maybe incontinence pads.

Standing by the door to the balcony is another semi-recognizable actor, muttering tired happy birthday greetings in front of someone's smartphone screen. A few other couples are roaming the room, armed with tiny crackers and large wine glasses. Neria and Taliunger are nowhere to be seen, but I sidle up closer to Eli, just in case.

"I'm so happy you made it! Oh my, and you're not alone!"

Ronit leaps at us from across the room in her dark, slinky dress, holding a glass of twinkling red wine that swirls and splashes as she zips towards us, making me fear for the fate of her spotless IKEA armchairs. Off-white can be quite unforgiving. She greets me with a peck on the cheek. For all its smudge-proof promises, I feel her lipstick smearing a clown-like red circle onto my cheek.

"Good to see you, Witchiepoo," she smiles at me and immediately turns to Eli, "and you too, Mister Witchiepoo." She holds out her hand with that dramatic poise of hers, and I can practically hear the cogs of her mind cranking and clicking as he shakes it. I consider her with weariness, *a twenty-year-old weariness.*

Eli stares at her and says, "Sheila and I are good friends."

Ronit's red smile widens into a devious grin.

She lifts her hand and performs the old, familiar gesture of running her fingers through her hair, and I smile at the thought that the gesture might be twenty years old, but Ronit is not. The dissonance is jarring, and the way she's squinting like a leopardess on the prowl makes me think that this leopardess might need reading glasses.

"Really really good friends?" she asks, and I notice her black dress isn't new. In fact, it's either terminally old or has suffered one too many laundry spins.

"Pretty good," he replies, and looks more like a punctilious accountant than ever.

Ronit, on the other hand, looks like a priestess sizing up a new follower. I remember how back then, when the group helped me land Neria Grossman, and we each had our distinct role, Ronit's only duty was to remove herself from his field of vision. *That's all she needed to do, just pull a Houdini.*

Out of the corner of my eye I notice a red-headed girl smiling at me from across the living room. As she raises her half-empty wine glass in my direction, she suddenly looks familiar. I turn to ask Ronit who she is, but Ronit and Eli have already disappeared.

And now, good lord, they're stalking towards me.

Taliunger is in the lead, dragging a reluctant Neria by the hand. She waited for the moment I'd be alone to make her move. *My God, my Eli, why hast thou forsaken me?* I want to reach up, run my hand over my hair and tuck in the loose strands, but a small voice orders me to keep my hand where it is. *No last-minute makeovers needed!* You're not some runny-nosed invalid recovering from mono this time, you're a gorgeous woman in her prime, standing here in the middle of the living room with killer instincts and a winning smile, waiting to bump into Neria again as if it hasn't been at least ten years since you last crossed paths. *But it has been.*

And here he is in front of me, and I sense Taliunger's body tensing beside him. I look up and meet his gaze; still the same lofty height, nor has his face changed much with those bright eyes, and yet there's no doubt this is a man in his forties. *And the years have not been kind to him.* As hard as I try, I can't see the boy I once knew inside this man. He's just a stranger in a living room. And was his nose always that crooked? I look at this tall stranger and feel nothing. And shooting into that nothingness is one distinct feeling: the spandex! First chance I get, I'll go to the bathroom and peel it off me.

But Taliunger is a whole other story: standing beside us tense and tremulous, her face twitching underneath several strata of make-up, her stilettoes embedding themselves in the floor, she looks like a tiny nail. She shifts her gaze from me to Neria, her lips ready to curve into a smile, but her nerves get the better of her and her mouth flatlines. She still doesn't get that I don't care about him, same as back then.

Go ahead, Tali, you can smile.

But, boy, did I chase after Neria back in college.

The whole gang joined in on the effort. "What are friends for?" Dina said, but that icy look had already filtered into her eyes. It didn't stop her from overseeing the entire operation, learning his class schedule and tracking his movements around his department building ("Hey, Neria, funny running into you here!"), finding out which protests he attended ("Hey, Neria, funny running into you here!") and rifling through the phone book for his home number. Naama was entrusted with emotional support, and Ronit? Well, as I said before, she was tasked with not straying, even by accident, into his field of vision.

And what do you know, it actually worked. The hunt was deemed a success. I still remember the moment when one of my idiotic excuses for calling him yielded an invitation to go to the movies with him. A movie! I couldn't believe my luck. But then, after a remarkably short period, came the moment of dumb dismay.

As we sat in his car, Neria Grossman confessed his unwavering love. I remember that moment well, the image still pooling across my mind. How the prey had finally succumbed to my weeks-long hunting campaign and said, "I'm in love with you," and "I never felt this way before." As the love burned in his fair eyes, I felt that something inside me shrivelled up and died.

All my feelings disappeared at once, like a plug violently yanked out of its socket.

Even in real time, while it was happening, I was already thinking: Sheila Heller, you're batshit, you're fucking nuts, what's going on with you? It's Neria! Your Neria! Your prince charming, the subject of your elaborate pursuit, the man you imagined, even if just for a fleeting second, as the father of your children. Here he is, sitting right next to you, confessing his undying love! What's happening to you, Sheila? Get your act together this moment, you basket case!

Neria continued gushing, I think he even used the hair-raising term "love of my life," while I sat there, immobile, staring out the car window. I felt like a doll, devoid of emotion.

And now he's standing in front of me with his Taliunger, both silent.

Taliunger is boring into my eyes, searching for something inside them, and I feel like saying: I'm not interested in your husband, just like I wasn't interested in him twenty years ago. *The only person I'm interested in is me.* But she pre-empts with, "After so many years, we all meet again!", cracking a big, smarmy smile.

"No, not all of us," Neria hisses, and his slurred speech indicates that the empty wine glass in his hand wasn't his first. "Someone's missing."

"Who are you talking about?" I ask, although I know perfectly well who.

"Queen bee, mother of all bitches," he says, "Dina fucking Kaminer. I can't begin to describe how happy it makes me to know that someone went and drained her, just like she drained your minds."

"Drained her?" a familiar voice cracks through the eerie silence.

"Drained who?" It's Ronit, wafting in out of nowhere, her cape dragging behind her, like a bat with a broken wing.

"Her, that bitch, Kaminer, she was drained. Exsanguinated. Didn't leave a drop of blood in her!" he exclaims, face flushed, drunk grin. Neria Grossman is brimming with blood and something else. A primal emotion. It's hatred.

11

A VEIL OF SILENCE falls over the entire living room, and it seems we have all transformed into frozen dolls, standing in a circle around Neria, who's still smiling and shaking his head. "Drained," he repeats.

"How do you know that?"

That detail didn't appear in any written account. I know because I scoured every article. I assumed she was strangled, and I'm almost certain that's what was indicated in the papers. When I mentioned it to Micha in passing, he didn't deny it. *But he didn't confirm it either.*

Dina's image flashes before me, baby doll in her arms, red letters marring that high, regal porcelain-white forehead, even whiter now that it was sapped of its blood. Dina of all people, Dina who had more blood inside her than anyone else.

"I have a friend on the police force," Neria says.

"What friend? Who?" Taliunger asks and immediately falls silent; a drop of red wine trickles down her glass onto one of the white armchairs, the fabric ravenously absorbing it.

"A friend, what does it matter who. He knew we went to college together, so he told me." Taliunger, who's already fishing a tissue out of her handbag to save the armchair, freezes again when he says, "He asked me to keep it a secret."

"Well, he definitely told the right person," I remark.

"It's the booze," he slurs. "Alcohol and I don't get along too well." He looks at me as if waiting for confirmation.

It's true. Once again the images from that Purim party loop through my mind, *Thrump, thrump!* Dina, impossibly tall in her flowing cape, and Ronit, Naama and me, her forever faithful entourage, and Dina's hands beating the tambourine, *loud, loud, louder.* And Neria, drunk, crying, angry. *Children don't cry.*

"That bitch deserved what she got," he almost yells, and this finally jolts Taliunger out of her frozen stupor, and she drags him away, like any good little wifey with even a grain of common sense in her head would have done the moment her husband opened such a mouth.

"Did you know Dina Kaminer too?" It's that quasi-recognizable actress, the incontinence star, and she injects her question with more drama with an appalled, "It's just awful, awful what happened to her."

"Yes, yes, awful!" A few other voices chime in, and the newly formed choir enthuses, "And that baby they glued to her?" "Dreadful!" "Horrendous!" "Disgraceful!" "Bone-chilling!" "Where were the police?"

"And for what reason?" It's that actress again. "So not everyone wants kids, why is that so offensive?" Now she waits for our approval, but the choir falls into silence.

"Look, don't think for a moment that I'm justifying murder," a round-faced guy joins in, *and you just know that any moment he's going to do exactly that – justify murder,* "but with all due respect, I think there's something selfish about choosing not to have children, and that Kaminer woman promoted that agenda quite aggressively."

"What agenda?" the actress asks, taking a step closer to him, "The agenda that says it's okay to be who you want to be?"

I observe the unfolding scene with boredom. *Here we go again.*

"The agenda of thinking only about yourself and the hell with your country!" The man with the pudgy baby face raises his voice, at which his wife presses against him and places a maternal hand on his shoulder. "Where do you think we'd be if everyone made that choice?" he laments. "Look who's procreating around here, only the Arabs and the Haredim, so take some responsibility, it won't kill you!"

A shadow passes over the actress's face. "I'm not going to have a baby for the country's sake."

"It's not for the country's sake, it's for your own! It'll be good for you to think of someone other than yourself for once!"

"I think I know what's good for me!"

"Well, with that attitude, what's the point?!"

"You're a guest at the home of someone who happens to think exactly like me!"

That shuts him up, but not for long. I keep a disinterested gaze on them while cracking pistachios from a big bowl and depositing the shells in my napkin. I know the arguments will forever be the same old arguments; whether the setting be a bohemian soirée or Shabbat dinner at your religious relatives' in Ra'anana, conservatism will always win. The round-faced man now shouting (because at a certain point the discussion will always disintegrate into a shouting contest) could have been Efraim, or the vendor at the kiosk near your house, or your GP. They all want the same thing, for you to be like them, to settle down, make babies, save yourself, themselves, the country, it won't kill you!

Maybe it won't kill you, maybe you'll just wish it did.

Someone cranks up the volume and the music comes crashing back into the room with Nineties Swedish pop sensation Ace of

Base crooning, *All that she wants is another baby.* Ah, Ronit and that famous sense of humour of hers. But where is she, Ronit? I cast my eyes around the living room but can't find her anywhere. How long has it been since she disappeared with Eli?

I feel the full-body shaper clawing into my skin and scamper to the bathroom to peel it off, knowing it would be easier to shed my own skin. But at least I'll be able to breathe again, even at the cost of visible flab.

I step into the bathroom, and what a surprise! Unlike the vanilla living room, the walls are painted a fiery red, and the toilet bowl is a shining, cold silver. On the wall to my right hangs a giant black-and-white poster, and who's staring at me from the frame, with all her diabolical splendour? Who if not Lilith, flashing her familiar smile at me, *Hey there, old friend, I've missed you, you didn't think you'd get rid of me that easily, did you?*

I carefully lower myself onto the toilet, keeping my eyes on the floor. I don't want to accidentally see the painting again, with that dark smile, those giant teeth, the red lips, the big hands and what they're holding. My mind is racing ahead, and I thank the lord that Micha isn't here to see it. *Not true. You wish he was here.*

Coming out of the bathroom, I spot Eli and Ronit. They're standing by the bedroom door, suspiciously quiet. I can't read their body language: it seems to convey both intimacy and detachment. Eli isn't looking at me, and Ronit is similarly staring off into space. I want to tell her I'm not into him and never was, so go ahead, baby, do whatever you feel like doing. *Just like you've always done.*

From the corner of the room I see the red-headed girl's eyes on me, and now she seems even more familiar. Just as I decide to approach her, I feel a strong tug at my skirt. I turn around and see a flush-faced two-year-old.

"Look, car," he says, one hand grabbing onto my leg and the other holding a big toy truck.

I give the toddler a perplexed glance. What is a sleepy two-year-old doing in the middle of Ronit's pristine IKEA universe?

"Ari!" Taliunger rushes towards the child. "You don't want to sleep?" she asks him, and without waiting for the toddler to answer, she turns to address the group around us, "We had to bring him along. He was supposed to sleep quietly in the bedroom."

I lower my gaze and consider this child, Neria Grossman's son. Lucky for him, he takes after his father, with all those fair curls. He's pulling at my leg again. "Car! Car!" he squeals.

I feel the piercing looks of those around me as I crouch in front of the boy. It's the same old test, the only one that matters, *and how is she with babies?* Each category will be scored and tabulated, I have to show just the right amount of affection (not too much!), straightforwardness (not too much!) and geniality (not too much!), but don't worry, years of practice have imbued me with surgical precision. I get down to business.

"What a nice car!" I say.

"Mine!" he shrieks and pouts. A thread of spittle dangles from his pacifier and Taliunger lunges in to wipe it, but pauses midway.

"Of course it's yours," I say and lean closer to him. He's purring with delight and beaming with puppy excitement, and his expression remains just as gleeful as he takes his toy truck and slams it into my face.

I'm seeing stars, flashes of light, and my nose feels like it was smashed to smithereens.

My ears are ringing with the sound of panicked cries as well as a few snickers. My fists curl into balls, pumping to the beat of the blood, *laugh, laugh it off! Never show you're in pain.*

"Ari! What did you do?!" Taliunger rushes to swoop up her child and begins to deliver a scolding, but I can hear the laughter bubbling underneath the admonishing tone, and soon the entire living room is awash with giggles. Now Neria is smiling, and even Eli's lips twist upwards, though he still won't look me in the eye.

I get up slowly, swaying solemnly, and stagger to the mirror. Other than a hint of swelling on both sides, my nose looks pretty much the same, but the pain is crushing and throbbing.

"Want some ice?" Ronit's voice cuts through the fog in my head; her eyes are red and conspiratorial as she approaches me and whispers, "Here," handing me a pack of frozen peas. "Poor thing," she adds. She's radiating genuine compassion, and just like that and all at once, I've had enough of her, of the sudden sincerity she manages to draw out of herself only in the presence of real pain.

That's it, I'm out of here, next time I'll know better than to poke and pry into the past. The past will always come back to haunt us, *although the thing that just whacked me in the face was the future.*

"Happy birthday, have a good one," I tell Ronit and turn to leave, but not before she leans in and whispers in my ear the words I'll eventually repeat more than once to the cops, to their sceptical gazes and endless barrage of questions. They'll try to challenge my account and plant doubt in my mind, but I won't budge from my story because I remember exactly what happened that night in the middle of the living room. Ronit looked me in the eye and whispered: "It'll be my last."

12

ACCORDING TO THE police report, Ronit was murdered shortly before sunrise.

The papers regurgitated the "in the dead of night" frill, and just like with Dina, they disclosed all the hair-raising details. And hairs they did raise.

She was found naked, tied to her white EKTORP armchair, *nope, not white, soaked with Ronit's blood – drained to the last drop!* – with a small baby doll glued to her hands, and her forehead serving as a billboard for the most daunting word of all: "Mother."

The detectives couldn't establish whether it was the same handwriting that had appeared on Dina's forehead, but the lipstick was the same hot red – the least maternal shade imaginable.

When I read that her body was found three days after the murder, the first thing I thought about was the smell.

It seemed like an especially cruel twist of irony that Ronit, for all her fancy Lagoon perfumes, Ronit, who always walked around in a cloud of sumptuous scents, was eventually found smelling what I can only imagine was less-than-fresh.

It was her boyfriend who found her, returning from abroad and walking straight into the horrifying scene that awaited him in the living room.

Even when envisioning the atrocity, I couldn't help but feel a bristle of betrayal. *Boyfriend? She had a boyfriend?* Later I learned it was one of those breezy, strings-loosely-attached relationships, with him overseas most of the time. And yet, Ronit had a boyfriend. *And a doll. See? They all get reeled in in the end.*

The detective duo who appeared at my door took me by surprise.

I was almost finished unpacking boxes, my hairballs ceremoniously resting at the bottom of the garbage can, *is it possible there were significantly fewer balls than usual?* I didn't bother taking down *The Witch of Endor* because Micha had already seen the painting, and its absence would only draw his leery attention to it all over again, which is the last thing I wanted after what I saw in Ronit's bathroom. And out of nowhere, *gling-gling* went the doorbell, and the detective duo burst into my living room.

She – a diminutive figure with pinprick black eyes and a ponytail. He – heavy and froggish with a fleshy tongue that looked too big for his mouth. I couldn't stand either of them from the minute I opened the door, and the sentiment was mutual, even if they tried to hide it at first.

"So, who do you think killed her?"

Just like that, straight to the point, no chit-chat or pleasantries. It was the short one, of course, her beady black eyes pricking the living room while Froggy plopped his fat arse on the only comfortable armchair in the room. *And it ain't a white EKTORP.*

"I don't know," I reply, "but I'm guessing it's the same sick perv who killed Dina Kaminer, right?"

"Interesting point," she says, leaning against another shaky shelf, and I don't dare tell her to move away from it. "Very interesting."

She drags out the "very" with a mocking drawl, as if she's watched all the same American detective movies I myself have watched, and I'm waiting for her to pull a box of doughnuts out of her bag and offer me one.

"You don't think it's strange that you knew both victims?"

"There were others at the party who knew them both," I say. Neria Grossman's and Taliunger's faces flit before my eyes, and for a split second, Eli's face flashes and fades, *just like he faded into her bedroom.*

"How did you know the murder took place *right after* the party?" Froggy interjects with a triumphant tone. The short one closes her eyes and sighs.

"Because it appeared in the papers," I reply, and for a moment feel sorry for the fun-sized detective who at least comes across as a sentient being, for having been partnered up with such a half-wit.

"So why do you think we're here?" she asks.

"I have zero idea." I also have no idea why these two are here instead of Micha. *O, Micha, where art thou?*

"Where were you on the night of the murder, after the party?" Froggy probes, and it's Micha's voice that rings in my ears with the words *the night of the murder*, but this time I'm armed with the right answer.

"I was at the ER," I reply. "I went to check if my nose was broken."

Shorty tries to hide it, but a laugh escapes her twitching lips, and for a moment she looks like Taliunger – just one more woolly haired gnome bursting into laughter at my breaking bones.

The ER is aglow with blinding neon lights as I stagger in.

Hours of steadily exacerbating pain convinced me that I better go to the hospital to see what the little heir to the house of Grossman has done to my nose.

"Yes?" the receptionist asks, without bothering to look up from the form in front of her.

"I think I broke my nose," I reply, and finally receive a look. It's surprisingly unsympathetic.

"How did you get here?"

"Alone."

Alone!

"Married?"

"No."

And no!

Later they'll explain to me that the receptionist's questions are designed to rule out the possibility of domestic abuse. Turns out they get quite a few of those around here, lonely women limping into the ER in the middle of the night, and the nose just happens to be the body's first line of defence.

When the X-ray technician asks me if I'm pregnant, I burst into wild laughter. The medical staff tonight all sounds like a bunch of nosy aunts at the Passover table. I'm still laughing when he fits me with the grey lead apron.

Tick-tock, tick-tock, no tot, no tot.

"Rest assured, we'll check the hospital records," Shorty says, scribbling something in her notepad.

"I'd expect nothing else," I reply.

"So, what did they tell you in the ER about your nose?" Again, that hint of a smile.

"It isn't broken," I say, and suddenly I'm sorry it didn't shatter and land me in a comfy hospital bed for two months.

"And at what time did you get home?"

"I don't know, it was already very late."

"Ronit was murdered very late!" Froggy stirs awake. "And the pathologist thinks that—"

"Saul!" Shorty shouts, and it's enough to shut him up.

So his name is Saul. Interesting – Saul and the Witch of Endor meet again, only this time I'm afraid it's Saul who has all the information here, not the Witch. *Use your famous intuition, come on, try to focus: do they actually think you're a suspect or are they just fishing?*

I try to pick up their energy, sense their intentions, but I can't.

"You really think I killed her?" I have no idea how I let that question come out of my mouth, *again!*, but I can't stop. "You honestly think I went to her house, stripped her, tied her to a chair naked, drained her blood and glued a doll to her hands? You really think I did that?"

Finally, I come to screeching halt, hoping Froggy won't ask me again how I know all that, and judging by the icy glare Shorty shoots him, it seems she's hoping for the same thing.

"Look," she says, "people reported tension between you two."

Big surprise. Ronit dragged my plus one to her bedroom, so, yeah, that could definitely cause what you'd call "tension." *But you should have expected it, Lilith will be Lilith.*

"What people?" I ask.

"People."

"So why aren't you questioning them, if they were so eager to give a report?"

"Don't worry, we'll question everyone," she says, "your boyfriend as well."

For one insane moment it seems she's referring to the palpably absent Micha, *and actually, where have you gone?*, but then I realize she's talking about Eli.

"His story is just as strange as yours," she states.

"I don't see what's strange about my story," I say, but she offers nothing but a small and highly unpleasant smile, and suddenly she doesn't seem so short any more. She keeps asking more and more questions from which I gather that they've got nothing. Zilch. Nada. Not even a lead to a lead. And when she leaves with Froggy, I realize two things: one, that she didn't tell me her name, and two, that the smell left in her wake, the fragrance now filling my nostrils, is Blue Lagoon.

Eli is so appalled he can barely speak. He hardly ever comes by, and his presence feels almost eerie.

This time I'm the one serving him a can of Coke and a few cookies (given the hostility wafting from the duo's direction, I wasn't about to offer them snacks), but Eli just stares at them.

"They talked to me like I was some kind of criminal," he says. "Especially her."

Poor Eli, torn from his peaceful life by two cops at his doorstep. *C'est la vie, my friend. He that lieth down with bitches shall rise up with fleas.*

"They didn't believe me when I told them nothing happened between me and Ronit at the party."

"Nothing? Oh, please," I snigger, "even I don't believe you."

Gone for half a night, locked up in her bedroom, and "nothing"? Who is he trying to fool here? Sure, she wasn't the twenty-year-old siren she used to be two decades ago, but her song still echoed, luring him into her bedroom like a sailor to a shipwreck.

"I'm telling you nothing happened."

"Chickened out, huh?"

The fragile male ego bruised, his lips pursed with insult. "Not in the least. I was totally into it," he says.

"So what happened?"

"I don't know, we kissed for a while."

For a moment I picture his hamster teeth bumping against Ronit's beautiful pearly whites, and try to imagine (and not for the first time) how he kisses. Probably with puddles of saliva, swallowing you with klutzy desperation.

He must have read my mind because he immediately adds, "And it was amazing. Boy, is she a great kisser!"

Irked by his little remark, I retort, "*Was* a great kisser, you mean."

That shuts his trap.

We sit side by side in frozen silence, and he seems so miserable and hopeless, like a sick, scolded hamster, *you kissed a dead girl*, that I take his hand in mine. It's cold.

"Don't worry, Eli, everything will be okay," I say, though I myself seriously doubt it.

"It was so weird," he says. "We started kissing, and things were heating up, and then she suddenly pushed me off her, collapsed on the bed and burst into tears."

"Tears? Ronit?"

"It all happened in a matter of seconds, I didn't understand what was happening, and then she sat up and motioned me to sit next to her on the bed and started kissing me again. She was an excellent kisser."

The pining tone is getting on my nerves. "And then?"

"Same thing. She pushed me again, and started sobbing like crazy."

I conjure Ronit's red-eyed image as she handed me the frozen peas. What I took for compassion towards me and my poor nose must have been residue from her little pity party in the bedroom, but what brought it on? Could it have had anything to do with what happened to her later that night? Was that the reason for her bizarre behaviour with Eli? Did Ronit know she was going to die? And then I remember, after I wished her a happy birthday, that bone-chilling whisper, "It'll be my last," and that mystifying look in her eyes. I wasn't imagining it. Is that what she meant? My head starts spinning, enough, stop it, Sheila, none of this makes any sense. *And the fact that she was murdered the very same sick way Dina was murdered, that makes sense to you?!*

Eli opens his mouth to say something and pauses, but I can tell by his expression that it's something important. I wait with an expectant gaze, knowing from experience that if I just sit here quietly long enough, he'll eventually tell me everything. But minutes go by and he isn't saying a word. And when a few more minutes pass, I see he's fallen asleep.

He looks soft and vulnerable like a baby, and I resist the overwhelming urge to hug him.

And once again I find myself standing and staring at *The Witch of Endor.*

The painting is right in front of me, hung at eye-level, as in every apartment I've ever lived in, always at eye-level, so I can see it whenever I feel a moment's weakness. *And so she can see you.* The Flemish painter decided to merge the Witch of Endor's image with that of your commonplace European witch. The result: dark, fierce biblical eyes with a pointy witch hat.

Help me, I plead to her voicelessly, help me like you helped me back then. She gazes at me with those dark, lashless eyes, identical to the eyes of the painted Lilith in Ronit's bathroom and the painted Miriam in Dina's study, and a small part of my brain remembers that the same eyes used to hang in Naama's room.

The images loop through my mind, four young women, billowing capes, toasting wine glasses. To us! The wine splashes against the rims, our cheeks flushed pink, *Ronit raises her thin white arm, sashaying on the grass, forever young, the beautiful Ronit!* Our mouths are chanting the same old tune*: Forever four, never less, never more!*

Now I'm the sole survivor.

13

I WAKE UP bright and early and can't move, it feels like someone has nailed me to the bed by hammering needles into my spine. I've experienced back pain before, but never anything like this.

While trying to prop myself into a sitting position, a deep, ugly moan escapes my mouth, *Watch out, Sheila, that's an old lady's moan.* I mourn the twenty-year-old girl I used to be, gone forever.

Somewhere in the apartment my phone is ringing, but I don't care, the thoughts swirling inside me are bitter and black, and I know that if I want to stay alive, I'd better expel them from my mind, but I can't.

My phone is ringing again, and this time I manage to pull myself up, but when I finally get to it, the ringing has stopped. When I see who called, I don't know whether to be happy or worried, but my hand is already reaching out to dial.

"Debby and Saul were less than impressed by you," Micha says, brisk and matter-of-fact. So, Shorty's name is Debby. Sounds about right, *it's a short woman's name.*

"And where have you been?" I ask.

"The investigation has expanded, so they had to put more people on it," he says, before pausing for a moment. "But here I am."

"They really think I did it?" My back starts throbbing again.

"What do you say I come over and we talk for a bit?"

"When?" I quake, but after a few seconds of blaring silence, I realize he has already hung up.

This time I have nothing to hide. All the boxes have been unpacked, and as I've mentioned, he's already seen my *Witch of Endor.* Yes, this time he'll walk into a (relatively) tidy apartment, with clean bowls, filled with cookies that *weren't* bought at that awful grocery store down the street. The only problem is that my aching back is making me drag myself around the apartment with stooped, elderly caution. *Really? You think that's your problem? Not the fact that all the others have died? That you're the only one left standing?*

And here he is, at my door, standing in front of me, with that dimple and bright eyes, those flexible limbs, only this time my heart skips no beats. When you're fighting for your life, passion is the casualty.

"Are you aware that you are very much a suspect?" He sits in front of me, waving away the (spotless!) bowl of cookies I placed in front of him. *If you must carry yourself like a bent old lady, at least be a good hostess.*

"Do you think I'm a suspect?"

I don't care for his silence.

"We've already covered this!" I shrill with a voice so loud it bounces off the walls. "It was someone who didn't like Dina's anti-birth agenda, and whacked her, and now Ronit, the same exact thing! Another woman who didn't want to be a mother ends up with a baby glued to her hands!"

Drifting into my mind is the image of a twenty-year-old Ronit, *forever twenty.* She's holding a brand-new baby doll, fresh out of its box, and hands it to me. I take it and smile at her, and we both share a knowing giggle, *while Dina stares at us from a distance. But now Ronit is also far away… very far away. You're the only one left. And you don't dare utter the other possibility aloud.*

"Are you sure about that?" His voice is sharp and tight.

"About what?"

"That she and Dina felt the same way about motherhood?"

"Haven't you read all the interviews they did with her?" *And all the ones they didn't.*

"Yes, we read them," he says. I don't like this *we*. I picture him with Shorty and Froggy, analysing the evidence with solemn expressions. "Yes, Ronit Akiva was certainly outspoken against having children," Froggy would state while the three pored over newspaper clippings. *Newspaper clippings, really? Everything's online today! You don't only move like an eighty-year-old, you think like one.*

I remember one of Ronit's very first interviews. It was after she had a supporting role in some trite, uninspired TV drama, but the interview she gave was anything but dull, including statements such as: "I have no intention of becoming a reproductive assembly line, I have far more interesting things to do," and "Childbirth is a national obsession, a cult that borders on terrorism. You're expected to have children, and if you decide not to, then society will treat you like you're somehow damaged. I am not damaged!" At the time, she got some serious PR out of that "not damaged." *But she sure is damaged now.*

"Ronit might have been very vocal against childbirth in the past," Micha says, "but in her last interview, she didn't mention the subject at all."

"Maybe because her last interview was after Dina's murder, and she was afraid to talk about it?" I propose, but then remember her hesitant reaction towards the young woman who approached our table at the café to pay her respects, Ronit's sudden and uncharacteristic modesty, how she passed on the credit to Dina, and even gave me some, *She was the one who gave Dina the idea…* Maybe if I'd paid more attention to this oddity at the time, I could have prevented everything that came after. *And everything yet to come.*

"There could be another reason," he says, and I can see on his face that he already regrets it.

"What?"

His gaze silently hovers just above my head, lingering on the painting. Still he says nothing, and my spinal nerves respond to his silence by coiling in unimaginable pain again. In an attempt to loosen my crimped muscles, I stand up, accidentally knocking over the bowl of cookies, which hits the floor with a *bang.* By some miracle, it doesn't break, and Micha and I stand over it, watching it spin around itself like a dreidel. This is also the moment I realize there's absolutely no way I can bend to pick it up.

Micha doesn't bend either. Instead, he looks straight at me. "What is this, some kind of test?"

"What?"

"Why aren't you picking it up?"

"Why aren't you being a gentleman and picking it up for me?"

"You answer first."

My mind strains to find a plausible answer other than the truth, but there doesn't seem to be any. "My back hurts," I finally reply, and witness a slight alteration in his expression.

"Oh, poor woman," he says, "I know what that feels like, really, I do." He bends over to pick up the bowl and the cookie shards, and I see how his back arches with elegant elasticity, opening out like a folding fan of healthy vertebrae. *Healthy and young.*

"Believe it or not, when I was young I had to wear a back brace to straighten my spine," he says, still hunched over the floor. I try to imagine him trapped in a brace, but my mind can't conjure up the image, certainly not when he's bending in front of me, all flexible and springy.

"What was wrong with your back?"

"Bad genes." He rises back up. "My grandmother had a hump."

I flinch, imagining that hump ticking inside him like a time bomb waiting to explode, if not in the near future then maybe in one of his descendants. *Blood never forgets.*

"I see that every time I come over I end up working as your cleaner," he says, straining a smile, and once again he seems like a vulnerable youth while I'm ensnared in my stiff, aching body. He takes a step closer and pauses. I can smell his aftershave, covering the subtle scent of young sweat.

"Where exactly does it hurt?" he asks, and I don't dare move or even breathe, *Is he going to touch you? Remember, it has to come from them, always from them!* We're standing at arm's length from one another in complete silence. My lips are located directly opposite his neck, but I'm as still as a wax figurine. He isn't moving either, and for a moment I wonder whether he's holding back because of his job or because he's just not interested, and this entire drama is taking place in my own head and nowhere else. I always seem to put myself in these elusive, ambiguous situations, but at the same time I always make sure there's some secret escape route by which I can explain to myself that it isn't rejection, *It's not you, of course not, it's because he's here in an official capacity, otherwise you'd both be rolling all over your couch, which isn't white and for that reason can never get dirty.*

*

He takes a step back and sits himself down in the armchair. When he pierces himself into the seat, his back as straight as a board, for a moment there he reminds me of Froggy.

"Let's review the facts," he says with a gravelly voice. "You had a big fight with Dina, immediately after which she was murdered. With Ronit you also had a..." He pauses for a moment, "disagreement."

"I see you're well informed." I can barely get the words out, still trying to process this quick shift in his mood. *Well, that's how it always is with these infantile boys, don't you know that by now?*

"In your case it's not so easy to keep up." He smiles again, his eyes soften again, my heart leaps in my chest again, until I remember Ronit dragging Eli into her bedroom, Ronit with the red eyes, who, by Eli's account, lay on her bed and cried her heart out. Ronit who was tied to her armchair, naked and branded with the mark of motherhood, Ronit whose flesh had already started to decay, the baby glued to her hands, Ronit who was drained of all her blood, *drained!*

"Say, how did they drain her?"

I can't quite read his expression when he hears my question; it isn't disgust, but it's something in the vicinity. "You don't know?" he asks.

"You know I don't."

After a moment's hesitation, he says, "They slashed her thigh, severed the femoral artery."

The beautiful Ronit, prancing on the grass, limbs intact... Ronit teaching me how to apply lipstick so it won't get on your teeth... Ronit that night, her lipstick all smeared... the rage and panic erupting from her body like crushing waves... and Dina looking at us from afar, like Miriam watching over baby Moses, stealing peeks through the reeds.

"So that was the cause of death?"

"When the blood flows out uninterruptedly, yes, you can absolutely call it a cause of death," he replies drily.

"But why the thigh?" I ask.

"Where would you have liked them to cut her?"

Where? A very old memory flickers and quickly fades, I try to hunt it down but my mind is already charging ahead and I fail to notice that Micha is still talking and I'm not following, until I suddenly hear the words "the group."

"What group?" I blurt.

What group.

"The only group I could be talking about, your college gang, your posse."

"I've already told you we were a group of friends."

"But you didn't tell me *what kind* of group." We lock eyes, all three of us – me, Micha and the Witch of Endor with her inquisitive gaze. *You beware.*

Here comes the moment of truth. Should I or should I not tell him? And like always, when a young man is involved, I manage to make the wrong decision.

"Just a group of friends from college, you know, nothing special," I say, and I am not in the least prepared for what happens next.

"Stop lying!" he shouts and almost knocks over the table, his jugular bulging. "Can't you see I'm trying to help you? I don't even understand why I'm trying so hard!" A tiny drop of spit lands on my chin, and I don't dare wipe it. "Sheila, you're rapidly approaching the point where I won't be able to help you, do you understand that?"

No, I don't.

"What kind of group was it, Sheila?"

Why am I getting the feeling he already knows? I hear the chant wafting through my head, *Forever four, never less, never more!*

"Tali Grossman says it was a serious business. That you had nicknames and code words, that you used to perform ceremonies like some medieval cult or illuminati-type shit. What exactly were you doing there?"

"Taliunger is a jealous liar," I blurt out, "she always was. I thought you were too smart to believe her wild fantasies. What do you think, that we pranced around naked during a full moon? There were no ceremonies." *Just that one time.*

And suddenly I miss Dina, who always knew how to put her in her place with a scathing look that said, *Taliunger, shut your fat piehole.* Who would have thought I would ever miss Dina? Who would have thought I'd have to bother myself with Taliunger again, as if I was still twenty? *But that's what you are, aren't you? Twenty. Or at least you think you are.*

"Did your group have a name or not?"

"It did."

The Witch of Endor is giving me a cautioning look, *Don't tell him, don't tell this man a thing!*

"The Others," I say. "We called ourselves the Others."

Once again, I see Dina's, Ronit's and Naama's faces, before… before that night, before all the deaths, paragons of youth and *otherness.* There's Dina lying on the grass, her hands resting on the small tambourine by her side as she smiles at Naama who's sprawled next to her, limbs loose and slack, hair splayed on the grass, *Naama's auburn hair,* and Ronit who's approaching us, arms akimbo, *hands on flawless hips.* Ronit smiles at me and wants to say something, but her mouth is full of blood. I open my eyes straight into Micha's face.

"And what was the purpose of this group, if I may ask?" he enquires after a lengthy pause.

Tick-tock, tick-tock.

"We thought... I mean, this freshman year at college," *don't tell him!* I'm searching for the words, not sure I'll be able to explain, *don't tell him!* "We took a course together and just clicked."

I recall the grey blob from the Women of the Bible course, the one who started it all with his *sages of blessed memory*, and all the mothers and children, and how Dina said without blinking an eye, "We'll have other ambitions," and we laughed and laughed. Because that's how it is when you're twenty, everything makes you laugh, *until it doesn't.*

"And then what happened?"

"We just thought maybe not all women have to get married, or have kids, or..." My voice trails off. "And that maybe we didn't have to either."

"And then?"

Don't tell him!

"And then, as you can see, that's exactly what happened. We didn't get married and didn't have kids, that simple." *I wish it was that simple.*

"But... but why?" His mouth hangs agape in enquiry, but he doesn't look so boyish and innocent any more.

"Because," I answer, "because we were young and we wanted something different out of this life."

"And did you girls get what you wanted?"

I fall silent. Very, very silent.

"Did you, Sheila, get what you wanted?"

Tick-tock, tick-tock, no tot, no tot.

"And maybe," his tone changes, "let's just try a little thought experiment: maybe you actually blame them, Dina and Ronit, the whole group, maybe you think it's their fault that you never got married or had kids, that you essentially wasted your life. Does that sound right? Only as an experiment, of course."

Tick-tock, tick-tock. We lock eyes. *Only as an experiment*, sure. Where's the "I'm trying to help you"? Where's the "I'm on your side, Sheila"? For a moment he seems almost enthusiastic, like any man about to get a promotion because he caught the serial killer terrorizing the nation.

"I did not *waste my life*," I say.

"Let's carry on with the experiment, okay? Look at yourself," he says and sweeps his gaze across the room, lingering on the hairballs lurking in the corners. "Look at your life. Are you happy?"

Happy?

"Is anyone?"

"Don't change the subject, Sheila. Are *you* happy with your life?"

"Would kids make my life better?"

"Let's assume they would," he says, and it stings. I reach for a cookie, ignore the dust sprinkles and take a bite. It's dry and bland, like those rice crackers you give babies when they're teething, and for some inexplicable reason, the image of the mysterious redhead from the party drifts into my mind, raising her wine glass in my direction. *Cheers!*

"With all due respect for your thought experiment, I didn't murder anyone, and you know that," I say. "What bothers me is that you're not considering that it could be the other way around, that maybe the fact that all my college friends have died and I'm the only one left means I'm next. Is that so far-fetched? Why aren't you looking into that?"

Tick-tock, tick-tock.

"We're looking into all leads," he says, but his tone says something entirely different.

"And if you're searching for suspects who knew both murder victims, then there were a few of those at the party. Neria Grossman, who hated Dina, and Taliunger, who hated both Dina and Ronit, and who knows who else was there."

Once again the young redhead's face floats into my mind, and I remember the glance she cast at Ronit who passed by her in the hallway, a glance full of loathing that lasted no more than a second. I didn't pay it much attention at the time, but now it's back with clarity and meaning. So why am I not telling this to Micha? Why am I not giving him her description? What's stopping me?

"I told you, we're pursuing all leads," he says, his tone oddly formal.

"You don't say, Mister Officer," I reply with a high-pitched simper.

"I do," he says, "and don't try to sound like a little girl, it doesn't suit you."

"You're right, it doesn't."

He gets up and stands inches away from me. "Sounding like one doesn't suit you, but *having* one would have," he says. "Would have suited you perfectly. I think you could have made a great mum."

And the moment he utters those words, I suddenly realize who the red-headed girl is, and can hardly swallow my shock.

14

I BARELY HAVE any friends. I'm not too torn up about it, but it does make me wonder sometimes.

Because the old Sheila, college Sheila, was one-of-the-gang Sheila, my whole identity was enmeshed and entangled with that of my friends, without any partitions or border fences. *What's mine is yours, what's yours is mine.* Today I know that's exactly the type of friendship you ought to steer clear of.

I do have Shirley, from the museum, but she's a work-friend, not the kind you actually invest in, even though it's exactly the type that – due to close proximity and shared daily toil – can transform into a true friendship. *Don't worry, that's not going to happen here.*

And there's Eli, but Eli's a man.

Even technology seems designed to facilitate my relative solitude. Uber reduces the need to rely on rides from friends (even though I'm starting to get sick of sourpuss drivers who moan when I type in a Tel Aviv address, as if I've just asked for a lift to the Bermuda Triangle), and the "handyman" app eliminates the need to ask friends for help around my apartment. I once tried asking Eli to come by and help with a tiny repair, but the bizarrely intimate vision of him labouring with a drill was too embarrassing for me, and I think for him too. I didn't give it another try.

I go through my mental list of "friends," and realize they're all dead. *Tick-tock, tick-tock.*

Now I pick up my pace on my way to meet the daughter of the person who was closest to me. *She was my best friend, but in the moment of truth, I failed at being hers.*

The Eretz Israel Museum is silent and still.

It reminds me of the Bible Museum, but a lot more formal and dignified; here you won't find the director scampering between the displays while barking orders (often conflicting ones) into two phones at the same time.

From the outside, the modest folklore pavilion resembles our wax pavilion. I almost expect the figurines to steal peeks at me through the glass panes, *You can't escape us!* But no, all I see through the window is the thick shock of auburn hair I should have recognized the moment I laid eyes on it.

"Hello there," says Gali Malchin, the redhead from the party. Gali Malchin, daughter of Naama Malchin, the fourth and my personal favourite member of the Others, the one who went and hung herself in her bedroom one day.

"I missed you," she smiles at me, and it's Naama's wide and gorgeous smile, from the days she still used to laugh.

I can't utter a single sound. All my memories come crashing into each other in my head. *The knife! The knife! Get the knife away from her!* Gali is still smiling, but she steps away from me and lowers a stack of papers onto the table between us. Guide fact sheets. I'd recognize them anywhere; they're always the same, whether the instructor is an eighteen-year-old girl doing her national service or a forty-year-old woman. *Tell me, that's your first thought when you see Naama's daughter after all these years? Really?*

She bends and pulls a heavy stapler out of the desk drawer, her movements as nimble and lithe as her mother's used to be.

I have no doubt that had Naama lived to maturity, she would have preserved her pliability.

But she didn't, Naama, she remained young, whereas we, the three Others, kept growing older and rotting as if it was our God-given right. *But now it's just you.*

I sense Gali's scrutinizing stare and wonder how much she knows. Something in the way her eyes narrow at me tells me she knows more than I'd like her to.

"Ronit told me you're in the museum guide business too," she says, her clenched hands stapling papers, *click!* Her voice betrays not the slightest emotion when she mentions Ronit.

"What were you even doing at her party?" I ask.

"She didn't tell you?" *Click!* goes the stapler. "I'm doing a memorial video about my mum and I wanted to interview her."

Click! Click! Click! The sense of betrayal resurfaces like a slap in the face. "So why didn't you come to me?" I ask, since I was her mother's best friend, me, not Ronit, and old rivalry that even death couldn't end rears its ugly head. Me, not Ronit. Me. Me. Me.

Gali takes a step closer to me. "I didn't come to you because I wanted *you* to come to *me*," she says and flashes that beautiful smile again, and it's only now that I notice one of her teeth is crooked, lending her an elf-like appearance. "And here you are."

The memories pulse through my mind, the plump baby reaching out to me in the dark. "Who wants a hug? Who wants a cuddle?" That tight squeeze, and those chubby arms wrapping around my neck, and a milky scent engulfing me like a cloud, and my heart opening like a womb, and there's that beloved smile, with the pink gums and that tiny crooked tooth, oh, my little, beautiful jellybean, you came back to me.

*

Three older instructors burst into the room in a frenzy of rippling scarves and rattling necklaces strung with chunky, colourful beads.

"That's our national service girl," the oldest one among them says to her friend, pointing at Gali. "She'll show you."

Gali raises an amused eyebrow at me and approaches the computer.

"Could you explain to me how to tag friends on Facebook?"

The woman making the request isn't particularly nice, but neither is Gali. While drily explaining to the woman where to press, she looks up and throws a smile my way. I return a co-conspirator's smile, but then remember that I get mixed up with those tags as well, that I'm not what you'd call tech savvy, and what's more, I'm closer in age to the unpleasant asker than to Gali. *That's exactly your problem, you're still clinging to youth.*

I take a step nearer to the table and freeze when I see Lilith's familiar face staring at me from the fact sheets. It's an earlier version of her, hair wild and dishevelled, mouth agape, toned legs and hooves for feet. *You actually thought you could get away from me?*

"Nice drawing of her, isn't it?" Gali's voice floats over from across the room, and if earlier I wondered how much she knows, I just got my answer.

She truly was a good friend, Naama. *She knew how to be one.* She didn't have Dina's intimidating edge, or Ronit's flirtatious irony. She was just Naama, kind and good-tempered, with auburn curls and a lisp, and that wide smile. But that's life, the good ones are always the first to go.

I consider Gali, who's explaining to the technologically challenged lady with the DIY jewellery why she "can't find her photos in her feed," and know that despite the physical resemblance, she doesn't take after her mother. I recognize her subtle cruelness towards the older lady, her convoluted explanations, deliberately making it much more complicated than it needs to be. I know that any moment now the older woman will give up and rise from her chair, and Gali will flash me that elfish smile of hers. I wonder whether I should be afraid of her, and whether I should have been afraid of her mother.

Thrump! Thrump! Thrump!

Dina's hands pound the tambourine, Naama's face is twisted and wet from tears. She's screaming words I can't understand, and the knife flashes in her hand; is it possible that Dina's laughing? No, she's not, her face is pale like Ronit's face, like my face, when Naama turns to me and screams, "How could you? Tell me! How could you?" and the voice isn't Naama's, but the hand holding the knife is.

"My group's here, you want to join me as co-instructor?" Gali asks, and without waiting for me to answer, she hands me the stack of fact sheets and as we make our way to the exhibition gallery, I notice that our steps are completely in sync, and wonder whether she's doing it on purpose.

This gallery is much more impressive than our sparse display rooms. Here they have giant vitrine cabinets exhibiting a vast selection of Judaica pieces, the neon lights lending them an eerie, otherworldly glow. The menorahs, shofars, candlesticks and Seder plates all glint in an ominous light, but the strongest light is shining from the direction of the amulet vitrine across the room. I don't need to look, I already know what type of amulets are displayed there, and I want to turn on my heels and run. *Is she doing this on purpose? Was it all planned?* Gali looks calm and composed, leading a group of religious teens into the room with an authoritative air, steering them straight to… wouldn't you know it, the vitrine showcasing protection amulets against Lilith.

The curator has chosen to position them by the fertility amulets. I'm surprised to find that there are significantly more protection amulets against Lilith and the possibility of her harming babies than fertility amulets that help produce said babies. But then again, fear will always trump hope.

"Girls, we're in Lilith's turf now," Gali says. "Say hi." The girls giggle, they clearly like Gali, who continues to explain to them in a pleasant and almost scientific tone about Lilith's creation in heaven and her relationship with Adam, and I'm rather taken aback to hear her say that "To this day, Lilith is considered the enemy of babies and the star of men's wet dreams."

The girls' ears perk up and the room reverberates with murmurs until one of them works up the nerve to ask, "What exactly do you mean?", to which her friend elbows her in the ribs.

"I mean that Lilith is considered a sperm thief, teasing sleeping men into *nocturnal emissions*."

Hmm. A national service girl talking about sperm theft? Nocturnal emissions? Very interesting. I catch her sneaking a side glance at the gallery door and realize this information doesn't exactly appear on the fact sheets, and indeed, when one of the chunky-necklaced instructors appears at the doorway, Gali immediately switches subjects and presents a conservative exegesis of Eve and Lilith and female roles and blah-blah-blah.

So. Gali likes to play with fire. I'm proud of her, she reminds me of myself back when I used to juggle a flame or two. *Back when I thought I was immune to burns.*

*

The difference between the Eretz Israel Museum and the Bible Museum has never been clearer to me. I hear the familiar human din of shouts, beratements and giggles coming from the instruction hall. The sounds become louder as I draw closer, and cease abruptly when I appear in the doorway. The silence is not the comfortable kind.

After Ronit's murder, Efraim gave me a few days off, "to calm yourself down," although to me it looks like the person who needs calming is Efraim, who's now looking at me as if he's just seen a ghost. (I know, I know, there has to be a better metaphor out there.) Finally, he pulls himself together.

"Sheila! Good to have you back. How are you feeling?" He manages to sound sincere, and a few of the instructors approach me, asking in unusually high-pitched voices, "Are you hanging in there?" "Are you okay?" and "Do you feel ready to give instruction classes? Are you sure?"

Only Shirley is shaking her head at me from across the room. She seems distant and I wonder what's going on with her, but not enough to actually ask. As I've mentioned, that's the kind of friendship we have.

Afterwards, on our break, she tells me the process is moving forward.

"I chose the father," she says, and without knowing why, my heart sinks. *Without knowing why?* "All that's left is an HIV test," she grimaces, "and then I can start."

HIV? Of all people, the innocent and phlegmatic Shirley has to take an HIV test. I'm not sure she's ever had sex. I mean, whenever the subject comes up, her stuttering, fragmented replies are so incoherent that I've stopped asking.

I picture her in that small, disgusting examination room Maor and I sat in when we went to take the test. It was early on in our relationship and it felt exciting, like everything else that had to do with him. Let's just say that today I see things in a very different light.

"So who's the daddy?" I ask, knowing I didn't push hard enough for an American sperm bank, the kind that would let the kid know who his biological dad is, would even let Shirley herself see a picture of him and listen to his voice instead of settling for the very basic and limited data provided by the Israeli sperm bank. Anything could be hiding behind such data. But then again, an awful lot could be hiding behind the man you're sharing your life with. There's no telling what kind of father he'll turn out to be, *just like there's no telling what kind of mother you'll turn out to be.*

"At first I wanted a blue-eyed blond," Shirley says with a dreamy, faraway voice. "The kind of guy I'd want to date. But they suggested I choose someone that has my colouring."

"And did you?"

"Yes. Fair skin and dark hair. A software engineer."

"Smart move. Analytical skills, mechanical aptitude," I reply with a smile, not sure whether I'm full of admiration or feeling a recoiling of sorts, and assume both are correct. In some way, the very *option* of having a baby via sperm donation is exactly what's keeping me from having it. If it wasn't an option, if that road was blocked, something inside me might have rebelled and tried to have a baby the usual way. But the mere *option* has set me free, *I am the master of my fate and steerer of my destiny, what do you have to say about that?*

We notice Efraim approaching and change the subject, although I get the feeling he knows exactly what we're whispering about.

In his distracted and discombobulated way, Efraim is *au courant* with everything that goes on inside and outside the museum, which is the reason I tense when he waves me out into the hallway with him.

"Are you sure you feel ready to come back?" he asks. "You've been through quite a shock."

"Ready, willing and able," I reply, and while I'm not sure I'm indeed one hundred per cent ready to come back to work, my bank account sure is.

"If it's a matter of money, we can sort that out."

"Really?"

"Really." He smiles at me. That kind of monetary generosity instantly rouses my suspicion. With all due respect to other types of generosity, this one is the only one that truly counts.

"Look," he continues, "I've been hearing all kinds of rumours. People talk."

"What are they saying?"

"No one thinks you're involved, obviously," he rushes to clarify. *You don't say.*

"But the rumours…"

"Efraim, has no one told you rumours are good for business?" I attempt a smile.

He doesn't return it.

"I do want you back, honestly, and you can return whenever you want, including today. I just don't want people bothering you, prying, asking unpleasant questions. I'm only trying to protect you."

And these words, instead of further arousing my suspicion, make me want to bury my face in his crumb-littered plaid shirt and cry. My loneliness hits me head on. I realize how much I want someone to protect me, and how there's no candidate who even comes close.

It happens when we step back into the instruction room.

One of the computers is open on the homepage of a new site, and I notice an illustration that seems familiar. The headline is screaming "exclusive details about the ritualistic murders!" But what is Lilith doing there, in that crude sketch? And why does she look so much like Ronit? And then it dawns on me. It's a sketch depicting the way Ronit was tied to the chair during the murder. The baby doll wasn't glued to her hands, it was stuffed into her mouth.

Yes, hog-tied, sacrificed, Mother Ronit with a baby rammed into her throat, and when I grasp the meaning of this gesture, my knees buckle and I collapse onto the floor; the last thought shooting through my mind is how strange it is that you don't actually see black when you pass out. You see a shining dark-red screen.

15

I DON'T KNOW how many people are aware of this, but fainting actually feels rather nice.

You're floating, suspended between heaven and earth, your soul is a flowing liquid surrounded by twinkling fairy lights, your body weightless, your spirit untethered and unruffled.

But then you wake up with a violent start, and that's not nearly as pleasant. And when you wake up to a reality like mine, it's *even less* pleasant.

Well then, we're past the point of denying or repressing it – whoever murdered Ronit, and probably Dina as well, knew the Others, knew *us*, knew *me*. No ifs, ands or buts about it. If anything, it's highly probable that he was at the same Purim party as us, drank the same cheap booze courtesy of the student union. He must have seen Ronit dressed up as the baby-devouring Lilith, must have watched her declare with a smile, "I am Lilith the Terrible, I am the childless mother who eats her young," to which we gave her our widest, teeth-bearing grins. That's why he went and shoved that baby doll in her mouth.

I have no doubt that if the papers had published an illustration of Dina in the exact position she was found, I would have known all this already, would have seen the link between that party and these murders. *And maybe understood in what position YOU will be found?*

I come to with a violent start.

*

Micha is eyeing me with scrutiny. Strangely, his presence is the only one that calms me, maybe because he seems so calm himself. *Too calm.*

Apparently, Efraim freaked out when I fainted. I was told that I was out for a few minutes until someone called an ambulance. I vaguely remember those moments of sleep-like haze that afforded my brief escape from reality, remember the flickering lights of a wakening consciousness, the inquisitive faces hovering above me and an authoritative voice saying, "Give her room to breathe," and then "Did she lose control of her bowels?"

That last question I heard loud and clear, and I think that's what made me snap back into gear. I reached a panicky hand towards my *bowel region*, and thankfully found said hand dry upon return. I opened my eyes to a worried Efraim who helped me up and also helped me convince the spirited (and incontinence-obsessed) medic that there was no need for a visit to the hospital.

Efraim told me to go home and "take as much time off as you need, and come back when you're feeling better," and I couldn't help but think, how convenient for you, Efraim.

And now Micha, in my living room, as darkness slowly descends.

This is the first time he's been over at such an hour. If I had a cat it would start running around restlessly like any other nocturnal predator, but I don't have a cat. *All you have is that broom over there, in the corner, and the familiar, calm Micha.*

But when he starts talking about the illustration of Ronit, he loses his cool. "We'll catch the person who leaked it," he fumes. "It could sabotage our entire investigation."

"Do you know who it is?" I ask.

"We have our suspicions," he replies. "We think he got paid."

"But why didn't you tell me that's how you found her? With the doll in her mouth?"

His gaze wanders to the Witch of Endor painting. "You know why."

"The only thing I know is that the killer knew all three of us," I say, and in the spirit of full disclosure – mostly because I can't be bothered playing cat-and-mouse games tonight – I add, "and he knew what our costumes were at the Purim party back in college. So I'm thinking maybe he was even there with us."

The long capes swirling on the grimy auditorium floor, the clinking glasses of cheap wine. L'Chaim! To us! Our cheeks flushed, Dina's eyes shining like diamonds, Ronit flashing her crimson smile like a blood-covered dagger, Naama harbouring a secret and me smiling under my pointy witch hat, smiling like I'll never smile again. L'Chaim! And only Neria is standing on the sidelines, eyes still dry, but not for long… L'Chaim, girls, to the Others!

Micha fixes his eyes on me. "If I asked you to guess who the killer is, who would it be?" His voice is velvety soft and I can feel him close to me, feel those breaths.

"Micha, a moment ago I was your guess."

"You know I don't think that any more."

Normally, I'd have something to say about that *any more* of his, but this is not a normal situation. I'm still weak and wobbly from my little fainting spell earlier, and being this close to him isn't helping. Panicking that I'm going to pass out again here in front of him, I clench my pelvic floor muscles as hard as I can. *That's it, Sheila, clench!*

"You're finally afraid," he says, still with that soft voice. "It took you long enough."

I want to tell him that if he shared some of my memories, he'd be easily spooked as well, but when I look at him, I get the feeling that his bag of memories is packed with a few doozies of its own. He suddenly seems tired and vulnerable. *Clench.*

"And besides, you have an alibi for the night of the murder, although I have to say your nose looks fine to me."

There's something intimate in the way he says this, studying my face through keen and narrowed eyes, making me feel naked. The face is the most exposed part of our body, and I feel my mask slowly slipping.

It was cold that day at the sea.

With all due respect to Dina and her idea to "cap off the night at the beach," Purim is still a loyal subject of winter's kingdom. But there we are, loud and revved up, shouting into the furious waves. I'm still puffed up with power from Neria Grossman's tears at the party, thinking there's nothing like the tears of a broken-hearted man, believing I'll forever be leaving a trail of teary-eyed men behind me, not knowing how quickly it will all end, and that it won't be long before the tears will be mine.

The cold breeze whips at my face, almost carrying away my pointy witch hat, but at least I have my cape to warm me up. We all have capes, each matching her own costume.

Dina is Miriam the prophetess, obviously. Who better to play eldest sister? The tambourine never leaves her hands, and she's pounding and pounding… It's a top-quality instrument, wooden rim and stretched leather, and she won't let it out of her sight, she'll keep pounding that thing *until she won't.*

Ronit is Lilith. As if you couldn't guess. It's not much of an effort for her. Beautiful and seductive, she's sashaying around in her dark cape, holding a small doll in her hand and every now and then licking its head, a gesture that makes my skin crawl but I don't say anything to her. Instead, I whisper to Naama, "Too much," and she agrees with a brief nod.

"It wouldn't have kept my dear husband from hitting on her," she whispers back, and we both start laughing.

Because Naama is Michal, King David's wife. My favourite. The small crown on her head complements her beautiful auburn hair, the reason she chose that character in the first place. The thought of them as two redheads facing off made her laugh. *But she didn't get to have the last laugh, did she?*

"I understand you went as a witch," Micha's voice snaps me back to the present. He's whispering, as if we're not alone in the living room. *He's right, can't you feel them?*

"I went as the Witch of Endor," I say. "I was always fond of her, of her unique gifts."

"And you girls chose those costumes because… ?"

I know he knows and he's just waiting for me to say the words, so I do. "Because they were different. The Bible's *others*," I say. "Miriam, Lilith, Michal and the Witch of Endor. Strong biblical women who didn't have kids, just like we promised ourselves we wouldn't."

But we didn't all live up to that promise, did we?

The sea is rough, waves roiling so loudly we can barely hear Dina's tambourine going *Thrump! Thrump! Thrump!* She really does look like Miriam the prophetess with her eyes steely and unblinking, and that drumming, which could have easily made her look silly, but it only lends her an air of power.

"Come on! Don't chicken out now!"

Who even thought about chickening out? We're fired up and ready to do our own thing, because we're not like the rest, we're not going to take the well-trodden path like all the students eager to get married during senior year, start having babies and settle down; we're going to steer our own destinies, we're not going down the baby trail, no, we're going to march ahead, towards... *towards what exactly?* A moment of hesitation. Ronit breaks the silence, saying, "Maybe we should take a blood oath?"

"We're not little girls." It's Dina's voice, obviously, since she never was a little girl.

"I have another idea," Ronit says and whips out her red lipstick. We extend out fingers, and she marks each of them with a red smear. Her face is screwed up in concentration, her tongue poking through her pursed lips, *a snake's tongue!* Her eyes are narrowed to slits, and when it's my turn, she presses too hard and the lipstick breaks.

"Must be some kind of sign, right, Witchiepoo?" she asks with a smirk, and I want to tell her it's a sign, there's going to be blood. But I keep my mouth shut.

I wish I could keep my mouth shut now, but I can't. I keep blabbing, rambling about that night at the sea and then fast-forwarding twenty years to Ronit's party, and finally I mention Gali Malchin, Naama's daughter. He's listening intently, too intently. *Watch out, Sheila.* But I don't. I ignore the voice. Because I'm enjoying this, enjoying laying out my memories before him like a display of precious stones. He's listening but his gaze is elsewhere.

"Why have you kept that painting for so many years?" he asks, pointing at the *Witch of Endor.*

"It's my second Witch of Endor painting, I got rid of the first one years ago," I reply. "There was a Flemish artist who painted the women of the Bible, like Miriam, Michal, Lilith… and we drew inspiration from his work for our costumes. A few years ago I saw this reproduction in the flea market, and it looked a lot like the painting I had back then, so I bought it."

"But why?"

"Because it's pretty, and it reminded me of things." *Things! It reminded you of yourself.*

"And Dina and Ronit also wanted to remind themselves of things? That's why they held on to their paintings?"

Wanted. The mention of Dina and Ronit in past tense sinks inside me like a stone to the bottom of the ocean.

"Sometimes we don't get to choose what to remember," I reply.

"There's always a choice," he says quietly, "even when it feels like there isn't."

It may not mean anything, but I suddenly notice his arm resting beside me at an angle that finally allows me to read the tattoo on his wrist.

"The fathers have eaten sour grapes." I stare at the text etched into his skin. *Of all verses!* The letters are surrounded by a reddish aura, as if he has just gotten the tattoo, but I know that can't be.

"It got a bit infected," he says.

"Looks painful."

"Funny, the first time we met you asked me if it hurt."

"And that was before I saw what it actually says," I remark. "No wonder it hurts!"

His lips slowly expand into a smile, and there it is again, that dimple flashing so beautifully between his light bristles, and I can't help myself, I reach out and gingerly touch the inflamed tattoo. His skin is warm, and I imagine the words scorching him from the inside.

"Why that sentence?" I ask after a lengthy pause.

"'The fathers have eaten sour grapes and the children's teeth are set on edge.' It's just a little *reminder*," he replies. "To remind me that there are consequences in this world, and that there's always a choice, even when it feels that there isn't. Which seems to be something you need to remind yourself of."

But right now I don't remember a thing, certainly not when he leans in and gently places his lips on mine.

It's not exactly a kiss, more like an exploratory gesture while we hold hands like a couple of high school students. *There was no holding hands in your ulpana, Little Missy!* Perfectly still with only our lips fluttering like wet butterflies, I wonder what now, and command my body not to move, because it has to be them, *always them!* And there he goes, pulling me into him, and I feel his body pressing against mine, feel that physical compatibility – you can never know whether it's going to be there before your bodies meet – our tongues wrestling, entwining, and I reach out for the back of his neck, which is something I wanted to do from the very first moment, only to feel him lowering my hand, pulling away from me and saying, "This is a bad idea."

Bad idea! Bad, bad girl! I want to tell him that he sounds like an actor in a poorly scripted crime drama, but I'm struck mute by shock, debilitated by insult.

What put him off? What did I do wrong? What? Did he not like the hand behind his neck? Was I too gentle? Maybe he was expecting me as the more experienced adult to be more assertive? But I went along with him, with his moves, in perfect, subsensory coordination, felt that it was what he wanted, that tenderness, *Well then, that's exactly the problem! Instead of thinking about what he wants, start thinking about what you want!*

The insult courses through me like lava, but I can't stop wondering what deterred him. What was it? I quickly go over every part of my body but can't think of an obvious culprit, so I continue ruling out possibilities. I showered after fainting in the museum, changed all my clothes – other than my bra, but it's not like he could smell that through my shirt, and even if he could, it wouldn't be enough of a reason for him to just push me off him like that, so abruptly, and with that trite sentiment of "a bad idea."

Suddenly Eli's face pops into my head, and I remember him telling me that Ronit also pushed him away just before things got hot and heavy between them, and I wonder if this coincidence means anything. I keep wondering and pondering and mulling it over, anything to distract me from feeling the full sting of rejection.

We sit side by side in ballooning silence, but I slowly come to realize that it's not exactly unpleasant, it's more of a to-be-continued kind of atmosphere, and just as I wonder whether he's feeling it too, he says, "Tell me more about this Gali person."

I remain silent.

"Doesn't feel right, Naama's daughter suddenly appearing out of nowhere."

Still, I say nothing.

"I don't believe in coincidences," he says.

"They say a coincidence is God's way of remaining anonymous." I just can't help myself.

"After what I've seen, trust me, there is no God."

Something in his voice suggests he wants a conversation on the subject. "Let it go, Micha, she's not your killer."

Are you sure?

"Are you sure?"

"It has to be someone who knew us from college, and Gali wasn't even an idea in her mother's head back then."

"Don't let her age fool you," he says.

"Enough." I get up from the couch. He tries pulling me back down, but I stay standing. *You won't bring me to my knees.*

"I understand it's difficult for you to accept this, but I saw the bodies, Sheila! It was ritualistic, ceremonial, something about the theatrical brutality was almost..." He hesitates for a moment, "almost kitsch. And the symbols, props from your costumes in both murder scenes..."

"What props? What symbols?" I blurt out. "I know they stuck the doll in Ronit's mouth, but what did they do with Dina?"

"They left something behind, next to her chair," he replies. "A tambourine."

I collapse on the couch, dumbstruck and drained. *Thrump! Thrump! Thrump!* There's something about that final and irrefutable proof that saps me to my core.

The thought about that small, vicious tambourine placed there as a clue – *for whom? for me?* – sucks the air out of the room. Micha takes me into his arms, and the tenderness of the gesture finally brings out the tears that were caught in my throat all day. He hugs me and pulls me tighter into his chest, and I can't help but think – so this is how he wants me? Like this? Weak and submissive? *Thrump! Thrump! Where's Miriam?* They're supposed to want you strong and mature like Miriam, they want you half-mother half-teacher, half-femme fatale, half-aunt, and you like that and you give them just what they need, *what you think they need.* But now you can't and don't want to give him that, not when he's holding you and kissing every inch of your neck, firmly, forcefully, and this time he's not stopping and he won't, and I don't need you all to tell me it's a mistake because I already know; I feel it with every fibre of my being, my teeth are set on edge. The sins of the fathers visited upon little old me.

16

When I wake up in the morning, he's no longer there. He did mention yesterday something about an early morning appointment, but at the time I didn't think much of it, still unaware of what the evening had in store for me.

I move slowly, my back starting to ache again, *but it didn't last night.* I sit down – carefully – with my coffee and replay the images in my mind.

More than anything, it was the tenderness that surprised me, and the intimacy. There was no mother–child or teacher–student dynamics, nothing that even resembled it. Although there was something there, lurking beneath the surface, something I couldn't quite put my finger on. And there was also that moment, in the middle of the night, when I woke up and found him staring at me with an intense look in his eyes. He looked like a big cat and reminded me of the time I housesat for a friend and woke up in the middle of the night to a giant cat sitting on the pillow next to mine, watching me. I screamed so loud he ran far, far away. Thankfully, the cleaner came the next day and found him.

You didn't scream last night, but maybe you should have.

The images keep playing like a slow-motion reel in my mind, fragmented seconds and sounds, and those warm hands. I let the memories have their way with me, and enjoy every moment of it. I extend a lazy hand to my mug, the one with the "To the Best Mum in the World" inscription, Maor and his insipid jokes, *Who's laughing now, huh, child?* I take a sip of coffee and pause.

You dumb woman.

My hand starts shaking, but I manage to lower the mug onto the table without shattering it.

Dumb, dumb idiot.

I start calculating the days, *the timeline!* When exactly did my last period start? When?

Mother of all dumb fucks!

I flip through my diary with trembling hands, find my special marks (my periods aren't as regular as they used to be, but they still appear once every month or so with dogged persistence), and there it is, the date, which now serves as an all-clear siren. Thank God, I wasn't ovulating yesterday. Or at least I don't think I was.

I lean back with a sense of relief, like a woman who just dodged a bullet.

And now back to the usual waiting game.

It's truly amazing how it never changes. Same stage, same play. In the starring role, the phone, now resting in my lap like a purring cat, only this cat ain't purring, which is precisely the problem; it's quiet as a corpse. And I'm waiting for it to come to life, because they have to be the ones to show the first sign of life. *Always them.*

It takes him an entire day, but in the evening I finally hear the beep of the incoming text. *That was fun.* I stare at the three words for a few long moments, and only then realize it's not the *fun* text I was hoping to get. It's an "I don't want you to think I'm a jerk" text, and nothing more.

Lighten up, Sheila! Stop being such a Debbie Downer, you did have fun together, right? Fun shmun. That text implies that it's going to be not-so-fun very soon. I read texts like the blind read Braille; I feel the text, I read the text behind the text, which is why I reply to this one with the exhaustive and profound detail it deserves: a winking smiley.

What can I say, we're the Sartre and Simone de Beauvoir of text messaging.

At least my conversation with Eli is more substantial. It's the one thing we were always good at.

To be honest, the bulk of our relationship consists of stories and interpretation, what-ifs and the advice we give each other. (My advice to him will never be one hundred per cent honest, given my secret desire to see his romantic relationships tank. Although considering my romantic track record, even my most honest advice probably wouldn't prove too useful.) When I tell him about last night and remember how he poked fun at me the last time we talked about Micha, I can't help but feel a little proud. But he's no fool, Eli.

"That's not a very encouraging text. And also, that was yesterday and he hasn't sent another one since."

"Thanks for pointing out the obvious."

"I've sent that text to a few women myself, and it was always when I wanted to be as nice as possible without leading them on."

"You're a real saint," I say, and my eyes wander back to my phone.

"Sheila, you're not going to obsess about this, you hear me? I won't be able to take it," he says, *because he could barely take it last time.* "And next time, if you'd be so kind, try to do without the pregnancy scares."

The only words my mind registers are "next time."

"So you think there'll be a next time?" I ask, and he sighs. "Don't worry, you don't get pregnant so easily at my age." It's the only instance in which the phrase "at my age" gives me a tingle of satisfaction, instead of making me gag.

"And if you did get pregnant?"

The question catches me off guard, it's not something he's supposed to ask. I start reciting the usual answer, but somewhere in the back of my mind, a black door opens to a staircase leading to the unknown… and *bam!* The door slams shut.

"Eli, I'm not pregnant."

You're sure?

"So you want me to start vilifying him now, or should we wait a bit longer?"

"Let's wait."

"Sure thing," he replies and winks.

I have no intention of sitting around waiting. Nope, not this time. This time I've got things to do, *things and then some!* I pick up my mute phone, call Gali and tell her I'm on my way.

Turns out she's still living at her aunt's, the same one who took her into her home after what happened.

I walk up the staircase slowly, each step awakening another memory – how desperately I wanted to go see the two-and-a-half-year-old Gali. How I missed her, her chubby cheeks, the way she pronounced my name, "Tila," with her sweet little voice. I missed her terribly, but couldn't go see her.

Her father, Naama's husband, announced that if he caught

any of us even in the vicinity of his baby daughter, he wouldn't be responsible for his actions. So I stayed away. *And there was also that awful guilt, which was entirely yours, Sheila.*

The door flings open and I find myself, with neither notice nor preparation, standing before Avihu, Naama's husband. *The widower.*

We eye each other, and the first thought that pops into my mind is how much he has aged. Avihu looks like a puffier and slouchier version of himself. His face is doughy with bluish-black crescents under his eyes and a mouth so sunken it looks toothless. But the blistering gaze is still there, and perhaps even more fiery than before. I always felt there was a certain violence bubbling inside him, but it was the pent-up, reined-in kind. Looks like the reins are off.

We continue to stare at each other, and I'm wondering what the appropriate greeting is for a person I haven't seen in sixteen years. Avihu solves that one for me.

"You?" he half asks, half states.

I try to crank out a smile but my mouth keeps flatlining. He takes a step closer to me, and I take a step back.

"What are you doing here?" He takes another step towards me, and I take another step back.

"I came to see Gali," I reply, and feel like I should have said those words twenty years ago.

"You're in contact with Gali?"

"No, not really, it's just that—" I start stuttering.

"Get the hell out of here. Now," he hisses the exact same words he spewed at us at Naama's funeral, in the exact same terrifyingly low and hushed tone. Back then everyone told us you don't judge a person in his time of grief, but I knew that's exactly when you should judge a person's character, because that's when they show their true colours. The truth is I had wanted to get the hell out of there, but Dina grabbed my hand and made me stay until the end of the service, until the last stone was placed on the grave.

And since there's no Dina here to make me stay, I decide to skedaddle. Just as I turn to walk away, Gali appears in the doorway.

"Sheila! Just in time," she says, breezes past her father and pulls me in.

I expect him to say something, to show even an ounce of the aggression he directed at me, but he just turns to silently stare at us as Gali drags me to her room and closes the door. *I see you even behind the closed door.*

"He wasn't very pleased with that, was he?" she says, flashing me that smile that makes everything look so easy and simple, and I can't help but smile back. If there's one trait I've always wished I had, it's that breeziness. But alas, I'm stuck with the gift of making everything more complicated than it has to be.

That was fun. Ha!

I'm surprised to find her room clean and tidy.

Naama was messiness personified; whenever I asked her to keep something for me in her bag, a leather satchel bursting with papers and God knows what else, I'd always get it back stained and grimy. But Gali's room is spick and span, despite its strange smell.

"Meet Jezebel," she says, pointing to the source of the smell, a red cage holding a small, trembling hamster. "She's pregnant, see?"

I approach the cage for a closer look, although I have absolutely no idea what an unpregnant hamster should look like. While I'm not sure what I'm seeing, the anticipation in Gali's voice gets me going. It always did. *Tila! Candy… you brought me candy? I did, but eat it quickly, so your mummy won't see…*

"Look how cute she is," Gali says.

"She is cute," I reply, "but I can't tell that she's pregnant."

"That's because I'm making sure she keeps fit. She's a new tenant here."

"What are you going to do with all the baby hamsters?"

"I'll raise a new family," she smiles, *no, that's not a smile.* "Want to feed her?" She dumps a pile of foul-smelling seeds in my hand. "Put it in her bowl."

The moment I lift the cage's lid, Jezebel starts quivering and almost pounces on me. *Why is she so hungry?* I stare at her digging into the seeds, ravenously stuffing her cheeks, and recall that time when I was young and offered to take the turtle from the school petting zoo home over the summer break. It wasn't long before I started to feel a niggling anxiety that something wouldn't live to see autumn.

Even as a child, the unqualified responsibility for the welfare of another living being terrified me.

"I didn't know your father moved back to Israel," I say.

"He didn't, he's just visiting."

And of course Murphy's Law made sure we'd meet. I wonder what I'm supposed to say next, but as always, Gali's one step ahead of me. "Don't worry, he won't do anything to you. Didn't you just see what a doormat he's become?"

"Gali!" God knows where this urge to discipline her just came from. "That's not nice!"

"Whatever. I know you never liked him, so don't bother pretending."

It's true. From the very first moment he and Naama met, I couldn't stand him. I didn't even attend their wedding, although that wasn't because of him. *You didn't get to see her in her white bridal dress, and you didn't get to see her dangling from the black rope.*

When their relationship became more serious, Naama and I started drifting apart. I told myself it was the price a woman pays when her best friend falls in love, but deep down I knew there was more to it. I remember the message she left on my machine, breaking the news of their engagement. Remember it word for word. *I can't believe I'm saying this to your machine, but it happened! Avihu proposed!* I knew the moment I heard the message that I wouldn't go to the wedding. I couldn't even bear to picture it. But it took me a long time to admit this even to myself.

"So, let's talk about my mother, shall we?" Gali produces a tiny camera, handling it with surprising skill. Did the hamster just let out a tiny scream or is it my imagination?

No, it's the sound of an incoming text. I never realized how much it sounds like a scream. I swoop down to pick up my phone only to see that the text is from Eli: *Well, how are you?* he writes, and I feel like killing him. I could murder anyone who sends me a text that isn't Micha. That's *how I am.*

And then Gali points the camera at my face, and I'm so busy calculating whether the lighting and angles are flattering – should I ask her to hold the camera higher so as to eliminate the double chin effect? – that I almost fail to hear the question directed at me in that pleasant tone of hers, "So how have you been doing in the sixteen and a quarter years since you killed my mother?"

17

I STARE AT HER, hoping that if I blink she'll disappear, or at least the question will.

But she's still here, standing in front of me with her pretty eyes, *her mother's eyes*, giving me an encouraging smile.

Just as I try to make out what's hiding behind that smile, my phone beeps with an incoming message again, and this time I know it's from Micha, I can feel it in every cell of my body, but when I reach for the phone, Gali barks at me, "Don't answer that, answer me first." Her voice is steely and sounds just like her mother's did that fateful night, *The knife! The knife! Give me the knife!*

But unlike that night, when I was struck mute, I look her straight in the eye and say, "Are you for real?" and after a moment of silent hesitation, the rigid mask cracks and she smiles at me. "I was just messing with you, Sheila."

I am not amused. I feel like shaking her, bending her over my knee and spanking her like in the Victorian novels I used to read as a kid. *Bad girl, Gali! Take that! And another one! And another!*

Instead, I say, "It isn't funny," and lower my gaze to my phone. The text is indeed from Micha: *How are you?*

Not again with this how-are-you business! Let me tell you how I am, Micha: remember Gali? Naama's daughter? Naama who was my best friend *and then some?* So Gali, who I used to babysit way back when, the Gali I loved more than I ever loved any human being before or since, and to whom I felt close in ways I couldn't explain even to myself – well, that same Gali just stuck a camera in my face and accused me of killing her mother.

That's *how I am.*

"Sheila, I'm sorry, it was like a half-joke," she says with half-remorse. "I thought you had a sense of humour."

Our eyes lock. *POP go the soap bubbles, bursting in my face, and I pull a pretend angry face, "What did you do, munchkin? I'm gonna get you!" I chase after her, but oh, no! I slip with banana-peel theatrics, legs high in the air, and get a barrage of soap bubbles blown straight into my face with that sweet ring of baby laughter. "What did you do to me, munchkin? You just wait!" And again, that tiny, heart-melting laughter…* Yes. I used to have a sense of humour.

"I don't get what you're trying to do," I say.

"I wanted to see how you'd react."

"Well, you saw." My tone is officious and pedagogic, and I see Gali has picked up on it, hiding the start of a smile. The corners of my lips instinctively curve upwards, but I pull them back down. *Not yet.*

"It was just to give the video a funny twist, and you're the only one I could try that with."

"Well, turns out I'm the only one left."

I can't catch her reaction because just then she bends over Jezebel's cage, looking so scrawny from behind, almost arseless with that baggy, dark jeans skirt hanging from her waist. Her flaming auburn locks suddenly seem scraggly with no mother around to make sure she uses conditioner, and I think of all those motherless years of hers, growing up with Avihu the idiot and that aunt who allegedly took care of her, but to what degree, if at all? Despite all this, she grew up to be this sharp and delightful young woman, and I think how proud Naama would have been if she could see her now, and at this thought, a treacherous tear starts tickling my throat and I order it to go away because I know that the lovely and witty Gali is fully aware of my terrible weakness for her, and I know she'll take advantage of it if I don't watch out. *Thrump! Thrump! Thrump! Take the knife from her! And that last terrible look in Naama's eyes, a look that said, "Et tu, Brute?"* The very same look I now see in Gali's eyes.

When I walk out of her room, I find Avihu leaning against the front door, looking weak and defeated until I notice that sinister glint in his eyes.

"I remember you vividly," he says. "You were the worst one in the group, she trusted you."

"I know, and I'm sorry." He won't budge from the door and I wonder whether I should call out to Gali, but I somehow know that she's hearing everything and choosing to stay in her room.

"Avihu, let me out." I take a step forward and it proves a mistake, since not only is he not moving but now he's close enough to lean in and whisper in my ear, "It should have been you hanging from that rope."

By the time I enter my apartment, my nerves are so shot it takes me a moment to realize someone has been here.

My home looks like it was taken apart and put back together; the changes are minute, but when you live alone, there are entire areas left untouched for stretches of time: a newspaper lying around in the same spot for weeks, a small mound of dust by the bathroom door you kept meaning to sweep up – suddenly the paper is lying at a different, straighter angle, and the dust isn't there at all. The hairballs have gone. It's the relative order that reveals the apartment has been searched. *Don't mess with my mess.*

My suspicion falls on one man and one man alone: Mister That-Was-Fun. I cast my eyes across the apartment, *Think, are you sure? Absolutely sure it was him? Couldn't this just be a way to vent your aggression over him ghosting you?* I scan the living room again, and there it is! The small pile of hairballs and dust under the lower shelf, the same one I stare at whenever I do my squats and lunges, and vow to take care of the next time I sweep – well, it's gone. And now I know what he was looking for, although he left the albums exactly how he found them. What's more, I know that he didn't find the photo in question.

I didn't take too many photos during my college days. Most of the time I wasn't in the right mood, and this was the pre-smartphone time, when we used actual cameras, so we only took photos on special occasions, *like a particular Purim party.*

I try to imagine my future selfie with Micha. Both of us squinting at the camera, our colours complementing each other, and I choose just the right filter to make us look the same age. *Keep dreaming, moron.*

Eli picks up the alarm in my voice and rushes over with a pint of rum-raisin, my favourite flavour.

"You're missed at the museum," he says, "and everyone's giving Efraim a hard time for telling you to go home."

I assume that by "everyone" he means Shirley and himself, but I appreciate the gesture.

When I scoop the ice cream into two bowls (clean ones!), he blurts out, "Should I get you some pickles to go with that, or any other weird cravings?"

"Very funny," I say, and realize it's the same didactic tone I used with Gali. *See what you would have turned into if you had become a mother?*

Eli takes the bowl with the smaller scoop for himself, and I immediately feel a wave of warmth towards him, despite his inane pickle joke. We never seriously talked about the whole kids thing. That's what's so great about our relationship, that we both know the limits of this delicate tango, and we each know where not to step.

But there was that time, two years ago, when his expression suddenly took on a serious note and I panicked that he was about to profess his everlasting love and crack out the old "why not give it a try." My mind started formulating retreat strategies, but he just looked at me and said, "We never talk about it, but if you're planning on having kids, I would be remiss if I didn't tell you that now's the time. I don't want you suddenly to decide you want one when it's too late."

I instantly blurted, "But I don't want one," and my voice cracked into a high-pitched squeal, and I realized that what bothered me was the fact that he thought I wanted a baby. I felt an urgent need to explain that *I don't*, that *I have everything under control.*

Since then we never talked about it, I mean, not overtly. *But in a roundabout, subtextish kind of way, you haven't stopped talking about it.*

That same week, a distant friend called to wish me happy holidays, and somehow we got to talking about kids, *somehow?*, and when I very casually stated that I wasn't interested in having them, a long silence followed. I'm talking real silence – without even the faint sound of breathing on the end of the line – which he finally broke with "So you want to be childless?"

The word slapped me across the face. Childless. The arid, lacking *less* of it. Childfree may sound like a trite New Age euphemism, but it's still better than childless.

And now Eli, with his pickle jokes.

"Are you, is everything okay with…" he stammers, pointing and staring at my stomach, as if he'll find redemption there.

Then it dawns on me that Eli is about to turn forty-two, and even if it all goes well for him, the possibility of being a young father is long gone, and my heart sinks. The decent, well-tempered line-toer Eli could have been the world's best dad, and I suddenly realize that he's hoping I actually am pregnant, because who knows what I'll decide to do with it, and what could happen along the way… It's common knowledge that in our generation there's no one way of doing things. There are many routes and detours and bypasses, which all eventually lead to babydom.

"I'm not pregnant, Eli, drop it." My tone sounds harsher than I intended, and Eli withdraws. I see his Adam's apple bob as he swallows a spoonful of ice cream and insult. *Bad mother.*

"Let's see if we can sort this out." Luckily, Eli isn't one for grudges. It's one of his nicer qualities. I, on the other hand, can let my insult (real or imaginary) ferment for years.

He takes out his phone and starts typing. "We have two murder victims. Both were turned into mothers upon death. Both spoke out vociferously against having children. Which is what we knew from the start, but then we found out they had another thing in common."

Did they ever.

"They were both your friends, both members of your Others gang, and this was significant to the murderer. He turned them into the same biblical figures they dressed up as for your freshman Purim party." Eli's fingers type quickly, his face screwed up in concentration. "Dina went as Miriam the prophetess and Ronit was Lilith. They both chose these costumes themselves?"

"Of course. You think they'd let anyone tell them what to do?"

"The question is if there's anyone else who can understand these allusions – other than you. I mean, I want to expand our suspect pool."

My ice cream has already started to melt, the raisins drowning in the creamy rum. I fish out a frozen raisin, bite into it, and my teeth go numb with cold. What are the chances it was all staged in my honour? *A diabolical play staged for one spectator?* My teeth chatter in pain.

"And what was the endgame here? The purpose of all this?" Eli enquires.

Yes, what are they telling you, these two dead mothers?

Thank God for Eli and his accountant's common sense.

Watching him type in figures and data, assumptions and theories, I finally start to calm down, imagining Hercule Poirot and his notepad, or Jane Marple and her excellent memory, but Eli and his phone will do just fine.

"Since the police focused on you as their primary suspect, it's possible that the murderer was actively trying to frame you, but not only are you off the suspect list, you even got a quasi-fling with the detective out of it." He doesn't type that last bit.

"Thanks for the reminder."

"Sheila, I'm going to have to hear so much about him in the foreseeable future, the least you can do is let me laugh about it."

I let him, and he carries on. "Another question worth asking is, why now? Anyone who has ever read a crime novel knows the starting point is paramount. So what was the starting point in our case? When did it all begin? What changed?"

Get the hell out of here.

"I'll tell you what changed. Avihu. That little shit is back in Israel."

"Avihu?"

"Avihu Malchin, you know, Naama's husband." And Gali's father, but I didn't mention that. "I checked, and he was in the country during both murders."

"Good job!" Eli seems genuinely impressed, and I realize how seriously he's taking his new role. He taps the new note button and calls it "Suspects," then immediately changes the title to "The Usual Suspects." I think I've already mentioned that he is a man of many fine qualities, but originality isn't one of them.

"So we have suspect number one," he says. "Who else?"

"It has to be someone who for some reason hated them both, and was probably at the Purim party."

"It can also be someone who was told about the party. I'm not ruling out Naama's daughter yet."

"Fine. Then add Neria Grossman and Taliunger to the list. They were both at Ronit's party."

They both also nurtured a secret hatred at some point, and both had good reasons. *Good? Excellent reasons. Especially him.* Although deep down, I'm slowly starting to think that these crimes were committed by a woman, something about the aesthetics of the murder scenes, the toys, the red lipstick, *someone here has been playing with dollies.*

"Anyone else?" Eli asks, and despite his professionalism and innate powers of deduction, I realize this is a conversation I'd like to be having with Micha, compiling a suspect list, adding and editing out names, rallying around a cause, *there's nothing like a common goal to bring people together!* But I know I wouldn't be able to have such a rational, constructive conversation with him. I guess it's true what they say, love really does screw with your head.

"Anyone else?" he repeats the question. "Look, I know it's not easy," he says, putting his hand on my shoulder, stirring up the memory of the hand that gently placed itself on me at the Purim party. The small hand of Dina Kaminer's brother Yaniv.

I still remember the slow, pleasurable crackling of electricity between us, until Dina came and put an end to it. Dina, who protected her little brother, *from what exactly, from you?* Just like Miriam peeking from between the reeds, watching over her baby brother floating in a straw basket on the River Nile...

"Yaniv Kaminer," I reply.

"The nut job? The guy who lost his marbles?"

"He's no nut job," I say, "trust me, he isn't."

Kaminer and his little hands. A few years ago, there was a deluge of rumours about him. He had left his wife and children, his promising job at the Technion, and become a hardcore Breslov Hasid. The kind that drives around in vans blasting techno music, stopping traffic every few blocks to get out and dance in the middle of the street. I remember thinking about him with a curious mixture of jealousy and concern, the same way I feel about anyone who steps outside the familiar frame of his everyday life, *How did he do that? How did he pull it off?*

Two years ago I bumped into him at a bus stop. At first I didn't understand why that bearded Breslover was staring at me. Then our eyes met, and behind their glossy haze I recognized Yaniv Kaminer.

The most interesting thing about that chance run-in was the fact that until my bus arrived, we engaged in perfectly normal, polite chit-chat – from the general "How are you," and "How's Dina," to the obligatory "How are the kids," and the perfunctory "Are you still in contact with any of our old classmates?" – never once acknowledging the giant Breslov elephant between us.

"Good, good," Eli says, "because our killer isn't a crazy person. He follows a strict, even obsessive logic." Yaniv's name is added to the list of suspects.

"You actually think he'd murder his sister?"

"I think it wouldn't be the weirdest part in all this," he replies. "Intra-family murder happens all the time. What doesn't make sense are the dolls, the lipstick, the whole obsession with motherhood."

I don't respond, still feeling the fluttering touch of Yaniv's small hand on my shoulder.

"He isn't the type," I say.

"Maybe he had messianic delusions and decided to purge the Holy Land of women who won't have babies? Maybe he had a pot-induced psychotic episode? I think that's definitely a possibility," he asserts and puts down his phone, markedly pleased with himself.

"Okay, I think we made some real progress. What say, Detective Heller?"

He digs out another giant scoop of ice cream and plops it into his bowl. I stare at his jaw working the frozen raisins and think to myself, if I'm the detective in this story, at least that guarantees I'll stay alive until the last page.

But that doesn't comfort me. Or at least not enough.

18

I SPEND THE ENTIRE way to the Grossmans' house wondering whether I'm doing the right thing.

Walking past the monotonous vista of houses, I peek into lit windows framing families having dinner, *The fathers have eaten sour grapes*, cottage cheese on toasted rye shovelled into young mouths, tables set with an assortment of spoons and forks, but the knives, *what about the knives?*

I glance up at the house numbers, steal into backyards, like a cat cloaked in darkness, to locate casa del Grossman.

Since I was never the proactive, probing type – more of a "sit at home waiting for life to come knocking" kind of girl – you could say I'm outside the circumference of my comfort zone right now. But then again, the thought of sitting at home, staring at the Witch of Endor painting from my armchair, waiting for the door to quietly crack open and for someone (could it be someone I know?) to come in and tie me (would it be with really tight, painful knots?) to the chair and glue a doll to my fingertips isn't exactly pleasant to entertain.

I have to admit a part of me enjoys this swift detour from the humdrum lane. Even going back in time to the Grossmans' house gives me an odd thrill; the thought of either one of this bourgeois couple turning out to be a perverted and flamboyant murderer makes me almost giddy. *Never underestimate the power of the bourgeoisie.*

But involuntarily, images of the future scene drift before my eyes, in my very own (unkempt) living room, *What kind of mother are you?* And I wonder how they would mark me, what gesture they'd choose to identify me as the Witch of Endor, *her powers gradually dwindled until there was nothing left of her.*

The first image that floats into my mind is me tied to my chair with a stuffed black kitten toy glued to my hand.

You think it's funny, Sheila? Good, laugh while you still can.

Turns out I chose a bad time to come knocking.

Through the closed door, I hear further evidence of the dinner ritual, the metallic clanging and clinking of cutlery against plates, and take in a gentle whiff of omelette. Herby. Then I hear a childish "Yuck, I hate that!", followed by a loud shattering sound and Taliunger's irate voice shrilling, "I told you! Now pick that up." I can't tell whether she's addressing Neria or one of the kids, since there comes a particular stage in every mother's evolution in which the tone she uses with her children becomes the very same one she uses with her husband.

I hear a mumbled apology in Neria's voice, and wonder when has he become so submissive. Back in college he was a red-blooded he-man. What is it about married life that turns men into doormats?

It's not marriage, it's parenthood. Puts the fear of God in them.

The doorbell produces the sweet, clear notes of wind chimes, and I picture Taliunger telling the person who installed it that she won't settle for any other sound. Only when the footsteps approaching the other side of the door become louder does it dawn on me that I really should have called first. *And it wouldn't have killed you to wear something more flattering.*

"Sheila." Neria isn't surprised to see me, and it seems he has no intention of letting me in. He's standing there with his many feet and inches, blocking the entrance. I peek inside. There's the omelette, next to a salad and a few elongated bottles of ketchup and other sauces. It's an unreasonably long table, currently seating three children.

One of them is Ari. I'd recognize that sinister, pink-gummed smile anywhere. Stuck in his high chair, he doesn't look like someone capable of, or even interested in, causing harm. My hand instinctively reaches for my nose. Neria notices this but doesn't react. Which is a good sign, because Taliunger's mouth would've already curled into that vicious little smirk of hers.

"Well, let her in already," she calls out over his shoulder.

Her acidic tone is surprising. I thought she would be happy to host me on her turf, a house smelling of omelettes, dish soap and bathed children, with Neria crouching on the floor, picking up the last shards of a plate. *Domestication process – complete. He's mine, honey.*

"Sorry to intrude," I say with my sweetest voice, "but could I talk to Neria for a moment?"

They exchange the kind of glances that tell me they've been preparing for this moment. *We knew she'd come crawling.*

"It's just not the best time right now," Taliunger replies, pointing at the table. I notice how short she is without her heels, cutting the figure of a tiny empress with her grand, magisterial wave, fingernails sparkling with metallic nail polish. *All this is mine.*

"I'm really sorry, it'll only take a few minutes."

My voice is quiet, my tone polite. In the realms of the bourgeoisie, manners work like a magic spell, able to open the biggest and baddest padlocks. Even the kids are listening silently now. Ari is playing with his fork, a plastic neon-pink apparatus, and looks dangerously close to shoving it up his nostril. The girl is cute, but her skin is glimmering with an oily sheen and I can tell she's going to inherit her mother's complexion. *C'est la vie. Blood always leaves a trail.*

We stand perfectly silent, engulfed in the delicate aroma of eggs and politeness. I can feel Taliunger's eyes giving me a once-over and notice her face is stripped bare of its usual mask of make-up. Her skin is thick and riddled with cavernous pores, as if ploughed by a thousand tiny needles.

"Fine, let's get this over with." Neria finally relents, and starts heading towards what turns out to be a study. I quickly follow, feeling Taliunger's eyes burning holes in my back, and regret choosing this grey skirt that only looks good from the front.

"Do it quickly," she blurts. "I need your help here."

The very existence of this study is surprising. *How many rooms are in this house anyway?* I know Neria is some sort of a high-tech big shot, and Taliunger does something education-related, *do you need to be reminded that you also happen to be in the educational field, and may very well have more in common with her than you think?*

But the modest dimensions of this room force a strange kind of intimacy between us. It's been a while since we were squeezed into such a small space together. The last time was in his car, back then, when my love for him fizzled in a flash.

"What do you want?" he asks flatly, but I sense he has rehearsed the neutral tone. I still remember all the different shades of his voice.

I lean back, *he didn't invite you to take a seat*, on a drawer cabinet without realizing it has wheels; I trip and almost fall flat on my butt, but Neria leaps in and catches me in the nick of time. It's a tight clasp that pulls us together, bodies pressed against each other for a split second, in which I manage to catch the scent of fabric softener from his shirt, *like a dog marked by its owner*, before we break free of each other.

It's remarkable how certain feelings never truly disappear; they merely ebb and flow, in and out of the heart, because instantly I'm overcome with the desire to make him like me, a desire to reignite the spark that flickered in his eyes when he held me. *Oh, no, Sheila, not that again.*

You see, I specialize in the field of unfulfilled potential. It's kind of my thing. Any man who has ever shown any sort of interest in me before, even if he has since moved on with his life, will forever remain in my secret pool of men. I still enjoy thinking of myself as someone's unfulfilled option, an object of desire. Eli insists this is the most problematic feature of my psychological make-up. "You like thinking of yourself as some kind of future possibility, but you can't commit, which is why you keep all your options open. But they aren't truly open, Sheila, and even if they are, they won't stay that way forever."

That's what you don't understand, Eli, it's basically Schrödinger's cat. Until you actually try to pursue an option, it's neither open nor closed.

I look up into his face, searching for that spark I saw earlier, *What will that give you? Don't you understand that's exactly what's keeping you stuck?*

"The night Ronit was killed, at what time did you leave the

party?" Uttering these words, I realize I'm mimicking the feigned intimacy in Micha's tone.

A spark flickers in his eyes, his pupils dilate and shrink, but it's not the right kind of spark. "What? Are you crazy?!"

I haven't even started.

"Do you mind answering the question?"

"You really have gone mad. You think I killed her?"

He isn't shouting, Neria, but his voice is loud enough to echo off the walls, one of which is decorated with a framed diploma proclaiming Taliunger a certified psychotherapist.

"All I want is to narrow down the suspect list, so I'm talking to people who hated us," I say.

"Who's *us*?"

His tone gives him away. Poor Neria doesn't know that pulling off a casual, innocent tone takes years of hard work.

"Who's *us*?" I repeat. "Come on, you're honestly trying to say you don't know who I'm talking about?"

He doesn't reply.

"I'm talking about Dina, Ronit, maybe myself as well."

No flicker.

"I'm talking about the Others, who else?! Can't you see we're disappearing?"

Finally, there it is, the flickering spark, and it looks like the right kind, but then he opens his mouth, "Tell me, do I look stuck in the past like you?"

A sharp pain pierces my side, almost making me double over. Taking a step back, careful not to lean on anything this time, I say, "It isn't the past."

"Oh, yes, it is. You come here, accusing me of things that happened twenty years ago."

How did you become such a loser?

"But these murders are happening now," I reply.

He looks at me with the same look Dina gave me. The eyes couldn't be more different, her bulging, dark cow eyes and his light, sunken ones, but the look carries the same sentiment, *How did you become such a loser?*

It stings, but I'm past it. Like Dina, Neria can say whatever he wants; he can keep standing in his study, surrounded by framed certificates and other visual aids illustrating his present life while the next generation waits in the living room, but he won't be able to escape the fact that the past never rests. *The past is the future.*

And it's this very insight that gives me the strength to go on and tell him, "Neria, you hated the Others, and you hated Dina, and we both know why."

I mean, now we both know. Because there were those two days when only he and Dina knew.

She obviously couldn't stand him from the very first minute. I never knew if it was something about Neria specifically that rubbed her the wrong way, or if she would have reacted with the same animosity to any man I took a romantic interest in, any man any one of us fancied. *Well, you know now.*

I remember her little digs, the names she used to call me those days, "little wifey," the snide remarks about toeing the line, wasting my life, "All your brilliant ideas, you know what happens to your brain once you take the marriage-and-kids route? And for who, Neria Grossman?" I don't know if this constant trickle had any part in my decision to break up with him. I don't think so, I'd like to believe it didn't, because when I look back, the first thing that shoots into my mind is that moment in his car, when my love for him… *Poof!* like a billow of smoke.

I told them before I told him, obviously, I mean, what are friends for? And that was my mistake, because Dina happened to run into him and beat me to the punch.

I don't know how it went down exactly – they each gave a different account – but one thing was clear, Dina was all too happy to give him the news of his own break-up. "You'll hear it from Sheila soon enough, but it's better if you're prepared," she told him, flashed her fake smile and walked away. Or that's what she said at least.

I still think Neria was the one who gave the true version of the story.

My expression must somehow betray my thoughts, because all of a sudden Neria flares up, "I've never met a bigger megalomaniac in my life," he hisses, pointing a long finger at me. "You actually still think I'm into you?"

Again that shooting pain, this time in my lower abdomen, and it hurts.

"You come here, to my house, smiling at me, begging…"

The pain is excruciating, I put my hand on my stomach trying to soothe it, hoping it won't start making noises.

"Who the hell do you think you are?"

You are the Witch of Endor, you are the Other, you are… You have a goal, don't let him weaken your resolve, you hear me? "But you hated her," I mumble.

"So I hated Dina for exactly two minutes and moved on!"

"So how did you know she was exsanguinated?"

Stop mumbling!

"I told you, I have a buddy on the force."

"What's his name?"

Stop mumbling!!

"None of your business, Sheila. If you want, get them to arrest me, but even then I won't answer your questions, only the cops'."

Neria's eyes glow like coals, *there's your spark, happy now?*

"And I have to tell you something," he says. "The years haven't been kind to you. I mean, maybe looks-wise you aren't that much worse for wear, but inside something's gone completely out of whack. So I guess having a family, kids, it does keep a person normal. No offence, Sheila, but you should get yourself some professional help."

The pain punches me in the gut. I have to keep myself from bending over as if I'm bowing to the wisdom of his words. *Who would have thought it would be so painful?* This usually follows a standard procedure: when someone even starts sniffing in the direction of my life choices, and seems about to start preaching or granting unsolicited, unwanted advice, I give them a very specific look or very specific smile that says: My friend, you go on your way and I'll go on mine, and just between you and me, I'm not so sure your way is that great, should we talk about it? Should we compare lifestyles? *No, they never want to.* But those words, coming from Neria Grossman of all people, caught me off guard, and the worst thing about it is that I hadn't realized until now exactly how far off guard.

I feel the tears coming and have to get out of here before they spill out. The last person I want to catch me crying is Neria.

"Thanks for the advice," I say, hoping my voice doesn't betray me, and out of the room I go, with the pulsing pain in my stomach only getting worse.

I almost fall on Taliunger who's been waiting behind the door. Judging by her expression, I'm guessing she hasn't heard the conversation, and I voicelessly pray, *Please, please, please, God, make it so she didn't hear, please, please, please.*

"What did you want from him?" she asks belligerently, without even a sliver of embarrassment for being caught eavesdropping. At least she didn't hear anything, thank God.

"Sorry, if you could point me to the toilet? I have to tinkle," I half-whisper, banking on euphemisms and general decorum to smooth everything over.

"Straight down the hall, to your left," Taliunger replies with civility. After all, the two of us share the same reproductive and excretory systems, and we're both civilized.

"Thank you," I reply, dart down the toy-strewn hallway and finally collapse onto the toilet.

The pain in my stomach worsens while I pee, and I'm hoping these aren't my usual PMS cramps slightly ahead of schedule, because the other option is too unbearable. *And seriously unlikely, so you can calm down.*

As always while on the toilet, my hand automatically reaches for my phone, where I discover a text from Micha: *We need to talk. Found out something about Naama.*

Well then, as far as texting goes – not a man of many words. Nine, to be exact, and five of them serving as an excuse for the conversation. I wonder if this is how it's going to be between us from now on, conversations that have a "reason," conversations surrounding the investigation, relevant, to-the-point conversations; yes, it's certainly a possibility, which is why the first conversation we have is crucial – it'll set the tone for all future ones.

I step out of the bathroom and find the Grossmans standing in front of me. If it was winter now, they would silently hand me my coat, like old butlers in a dilapidated Victorian mansion. He seems tired and she looks vexed. He starts to say something, but she shushes him.

Outside, my phone rings and I'm so sure it's Micha that I don't even bother to look at the name flashing on the screen, but when I pick up, it's Gali, and she's so upset I can barely understand a word she's saying.

"Jezebel's giving birth," she says, "and I think there's a problem."

The distress in her voice is so palpable that I immediately ask if she wants me to come over, even though I have no doubt it's going to be disgusting, and bloody. *All that goopy slime that is the miracle of birth.*

"Yes," she whimpers, "please come."

She quickly opens the door, flustered and bleary-eyed. The house is quiet, and there's no sign of Avihu. *With such clear signs of new life, is it any wonder the widower has disappeared?*

As soon as I open the door to her room, the smell smacks me in the face, red and metallic. I turn my gaze in the direction of the cage but can hardly see a thing; it's all stuffed with wads of torn toilet paper.

"I followed all the instructions," Gali says, "come, look."

I approach the cage and see Jezebel with two red, moist lumps by her side. Only one of them is moving.

"It said not to touch them," she says, "I think they'll be okay, but look at Jezebel."

The hamster isn't moving. A grey, eyeless blob, she looks like a taxidermied gremlin. "It isn't supposed to be like this after the birth, I saw a video on YouTube."

"Is it over?" I ask.

"I'm not sure, there might be one still stuck inside."

"Can't you check? Maybe call a vet?"

"I don't know... I wasn't thinking straight," she falters, "I just called you. I don't know why I'm being such an idiot."

I know why. And I want to hug her, but I don't dare. *And how would you?*

"Look at them, they're so tiny, they might not even make it. They might die. She might die..." Her voice trails off, and just then Jezebel opens her eyes. She isn't moving, but seems aware of what's happening in the room.

"I barely remember Mali." Gali's voice is so quiet, I have to move closer to hear her. "I remember my mum well, and also think about her a lot, but I barely have any memories of Mali. Isn't that weird? Twins are supposed to be so close..."

Gali is still facing the cage, with me behind her, my hand on her shoulder, *how is your hand not bursting into flames?* Both of us silent, I can sense her tears before she lets out the first sob.

"You know that if Jezebel doesn't die, there's a chance she might eat her babies? That's how it is with hamsters." Her voice is wet, and I know what she's going to say next, and freeze. "And not just with hamsters, apparently."

"Oh, Gali, honey, don't," I tell her, and just then, I hear a sharp, scary squeal and the cage starts to shake. I try to see what's going on, but Gali is blocking my view of Jezebel, and I don't dare move, not a millimetre. She's crying her eyes out now, *these are old tears.*

"They say Mali was the first, that Mum strangled her first, and then when she got to me, she ran out of strength in the middle. But how hard could it be to strangle a two-and-a-half-year-old?"

Naama's face drifts into my mind, a small crown sparkling on her head; she's trying to tell me something but can't get the words out. When Gali turns to me, her face is red and contorted, *she doesn't look like her, she doesn't.* I hug her, feel her small head on my shoulder and so want to cry along with her, but I know I don't have the right.

"There, there, little munchkin, shh..." I try soothing her as if she were a little girl. *She never was a little girl, never got the chance.*

"She had enough strength to hang herself afterwards, had enough strength for that," she says with a muffled voice, head still pressed into my shoulder. "They said I was a medical miracle, that I was lucky to come out of it without brain damage..."

"Sweetheart..." I rock her back and forth but her body is stiff and unyielding, *or maybe you just don't know how to do this? Maybe you don't know how to calm an upset child?*

"You see, Sheila? A mum who tries to choke you to death, who strangles your twin sister and commits suicide, but I'm lucky because I don't have brain damage..."

And finally, she breaks down in my arms and I hug her tighter, pressing her against me, my shirt wet with tears, or saliva, or snot, and I'm surprised to find myself undeterred and undisgusted, maybe even the opposite. From deep within me the old sing-songy call rises, *Little munchkin, pretty little munchkin, who wants a hug? Who? Here she is, coming to her Auntie Sheila...* Gali's sobs become louder, blending with the tiny shrieks coming from cage, and then there's nothing but silence.

19

I DREAM ABOUT NAAMA.

I know it's a dream, because I can hear my own voice saying, "This isn't a bad dream, Sheila, you could have had nightmares, but this isn't a bad dream." I see the red-headed girl, her face round and cherubic, without even a single tiny freckle to mar the skin, and she's prancing towards me, her steps light and breezy despite the black rope wrapped around her neck, dragging behind her on the grass. She approaches me and almost touches my face, *don't touch my face!* But the rope stops her short. That's when I wake up.

And there's the other dream. The red hair shorter, the face not so cherubic any more. She's sitting on a swing, holding the chains, knuckles white with effort, *the chains black.* She's swinging back and forth with momentum. Two little girls are sitting at her feet, and I know it's Gali and Mali, even though they look like a weird, squished version of themselves. Gali has no feet and Mali is transparent, I can see the trees through her.

The two toddlers press their foreheads together and giggle; then Naama joins them and they all laugh with big, gaping mouths, and I think to myself: this is a dream. This has to be a dream, because I never saw Naama laughing with her daughters like that. I'll never forget that look she'd get in her eyes whenever one of them called her "Mum."

And now, pull yourself together and tidy up the place for Micha.

Part of me wonders, why bother? If he's the one who searched my place earlier, then he already saw the mess, all the spots and stains I'm now trying to hide. But another, more adamant part of me wants him to find the house spick and span and lemony-fresh. *A mother's house.*

And herein lies the problem. In my day-to-day life, I try to steer clear of responsibility, commitment and order, but every time a new relationship starts, or I even just sense I see one coming, the "mummy" immediately emerges from within me. Like with Maor, when picking up his socks or surprising him with a new dish became the highlight of my day.

And the strangest part of it all is that I actually enjoy it. The housework, even the most tedious of chores, even the kind that ruin your delicate hands, suddenly take on meaning, become an important part of the package deal that defines a budding relationship. *But you don't really know how to be a mummy, so your kids feel cheated.*

My body is still tense, my stomach pulsing with strange, muffled beats.

I stretch out, whirling around the house like a spinning top, looking to release all that pent-up energy, washing dishes with rubber gloves, *protect the skin on your hands*, combatting stubborn stains with Dettol wipes, dusting sooty surfaces. But I keep dropping everything, from the small, filthy scouring pad to the "Best Mum in the World" mug. I pick up the pieces, careful not to nick myself, my hands heavy and weak. *Your body's talking to you, listen.*

My lower abdomen is so bloated it feels like the waistband of my pants might snap, but there's nothing left for me to do but wait. Gone are the days when you could set a watch by my period, now I just have to wait patiently for whenever it comes. *And hope it decides to visit again.* The pesky voice in the back of my mind is whispering something else to me, but I tell it to shut up. The only thing I care about right now are the dynamics soon to be established between me and Micha here in my living room, which will hopefully be clean and tidy by then. You can't underestimate the importance of the first encounter after a first fling, and it can go either way.

I try to come up with opening lines, possible topics of conversation that will cast me in a flattering light, *oh, come on, you big baby, you're past that stage,* I even zero in on the exact angle I'll be sitting at when I call out, "It's open!" and he'll walk through the door – my head ever so slightly tilted, hair casually but seductively pouring down my shoulder. But deep down I know everything will rise and fall on the first "hello."

He doesn't bother to say hello.

He just barges in and makes a beeline for the bedroom, or at least that's how it appears. I immediately wonder how I should react to this rush of desire, when he pauses in the hallway in front of the painting of the Witch of Endor.

"Did Naama have one of these paintings too?" he asks.

I approach him, trying to sense his magnetic field, but all he gives off is the smell of sweat. Unlike the other times, the scent makes me take a step back, and I wonder if it's because I'm sensing imminent rejection and trying to protect myself.

"She had a small reproduction when we were in college," I reply, "but I don't think she kept it."

"Why not?"

Because.

"She got married senior year, Micha, that's why. The painting wasn't relevant to her life any more, maybe it even annoyed her."

But not as much as she annoyed us during those confusing, early days of her relationship with Avihu. I remember the acid that crept up my throat after every good date she had, and the moment of realization that this was it, she's going to marry him. I also remember Dina's complete disbelief. But I knew it was going to happen, felt it in my bones. My envy was visceral, and the signs were in the air. It's a miracle we managed to get over it and stay friends. *That's because you weren't jealous of her for the usual reasons.*

But Dina wouldn't relent. "You're marrying him because you're pregnant, aren't you?" she asked her, to which Naama calmly replied, "I'm not. Not yet. But I will be soon."

No, that wasn't the right thing to say to Dina Kaminer.

Micha continues to study the painting, and I'm wondering whether it's because he doesn't want to look me in the eye.

"If the killer had wanted to mark Naama as the character from her costume, what would he have done to her?"

I can't remember ever seeing him this focused. His face is so close to the painting it looks like he's going to kiss it. *And, boy, is he good at that.*

"Well?" He takes a step closer to me. Now I can pick up his energy. I like the way his T-shirt clings to his body, which I can now describe in intimate detail. I inch towards him, but he doesn't notice, or at least pretends not to.

"You said you have photos from that Purim party, where are they? They might tell us something about her costume."

His gaze scours the living room, knowing just where to look. *You won't find them, Mister Detective!*

He keeps studying the living room with his expert gaze, sifting and surveying, and I suddenly realize how cramped and shabby it is, filled with second-hand furniture from friends, bulky, heavy pieces that aren't even remotely my taste. What's more, it dawns on me how many times I've moved, always settling for the leftover furnishings of others, and that I don't even know what my own style is. Or if I even have one.

"Fuck the costume," I say.

"What did you say?" He's surprised.

"Exactly what you heard," I reply. "That's it? This is how it's going to be from now on? You're the detective and I give you information, as if nothing happened between us?"

I have to keep myself from crying. Tears never did work in my favour. *You're a strong woman.*

"Come on, Sheila." He's finally looking at me – the same scrutinizing gaze with which he just dissected the painting. Whatever he finds in my face makes him sit down on the couch and pull me towards him, but when I hold on to him and try to bury my face in the crook of his neck, he pushes me away.

"Look, I'm attracted to you," he says, and my heart sinks. That's the worst thing a man can say to a woman, because it always foreshadows a crash and burn. "But we both know it's not that simple."

Well, there you have it. Crash. Burn.

"We just got carried away… obviously, I don't regret it." He smiles, and it's the same knowing smile he gave me a moment before he got out of bed, *leaving you there bewildered and beguiled.*

I don't return the smile, even though I know I should. I should give him the widest, coldest smile I can muster. *Don't make a fuss, you're not a child.*

"Come on, Sheila, I'd be in serious trouble if they found out on the force, you know it's tricky."

Oh, so now it's "tricky." For a moment I think he's going to suggest we "keep it under the radar," and I can already feel myself recoiling with humiliation, but he doesn't. He's no fool, Micha. *He's a smart boy.*

You see, I already know all there is to know about under-the-radar love stories.

I was twenty-five and he was thirty-seven, very charming, and very married. *You naïve, silly girl!* The affair lasted a few months and the only good thing that came out of it is that at twenty-five, I was safely and permanently out of danger of ever falling in love with a married man again. And the danger was real. These married men, secular or religious, are insatiable.

The tables have since turned, obviously. Today I'm the older woman, but these young men that I'm so partial to are not the least bit naïve.

And again my body aches with restlessness. I can't keep sitting next to him like this, it's making my bones hurt. I'm overwhelmed with a desperate need to busy my hands, to turn on faucets, fill bowls, *smash plates into a thousand pieces! To roar into the wind!* Anything but keep sitting here like a dummy on the couch.

I retreat to the kitchen to whip up something to eat: I'm thinking salad. Chop some white cabbage, sprinkle dried cranberries on top, *and voila, a dash of elegant hosting!* But the cranberries in the fridge are so old they've fused into a rock-hard mess. They look like a giant blood clot.

I return to the living room with a pile of sticky date-filled cookies and salty pretzels, which Micha probably won't eat, but I enjoy placing them in front of him, on the small table.

"Looks good," he says, picking up a cookie. He puts it in his mouth, starts chewing and keeps chewing for some time, as if the oral effort signifies a special peace offering.

"Yumm," he says, and swallows with some difficulty. "Let's talk business for a moment, Sheila. How could the killer have marked Naama as Michal, King David's wife?"

"I have no idea," I reply. "Maybe he put a crown on her head."

"No, there was no crown."

For a moment I wonder whether Michal committed suicide with her crown on. *The queen will always be the one to lose her head.*

"Enough with the games. What did you find out?"

"I'll tell you what we found out," he says, and swallows. "Turns out that black rope they kept mentioning wasn't a rope at all. It was a tefillin set. Naama went and hanged herself with Avihu's tefillin."

My head is spinning.

I imagine the black leather straps cutting deep into her flesh, more painful than any rope. Especially for Naama with that delicate white neck of hers, *women's skin isn't made for tefillin.*

I remember the grey blob's Bible lecture – the only one we attended before dropping his course, before becoming the Others – in which he mentioned that according to biblical exegesis, Michal, King David's wife, used to lay tefillin – a strictly male business. I personally never felt the need to wind leather straps around my arm, but hey, to each her own. He then declared that certain Judaic authorities believed the core of her soul to be masculine, "and that's why…" he stated with much fanfare, and the only time during the entire lecture that his grey cheeks looked almost rosy, "that's why Michal didn't have kids."

The loud snort of disdain came from Naama.

"Do you understand what that means?" Micha asks, and for one crazy moment, I think he's about to say Naama is the killer, that she's the one murdering all the Others and gluing dolls to their hands, *Naama roaring from inside her grave, Naama crying the lament of the empty womb*, but that moment quickly passes, leaving me shuddering for an entirely different reason, because Micha looks at me and says, "It means it's very possible that the first member of the Others was murdered sixteen years ago."

20

THE FATHERS *have eaten sour grapes.* Micha's tattooed arm is resting next to me on the couch.

I feel a strange dullness, as if this new information I've been given has somehow rearranged the molecules in my body. We're all merely the sum of our experiences and memories, and the moment we are made to reconsider important information that has lain deep and unquestioned inside us for so long, our body, our entire self, has to realign itself accordingly.

I stare at his tattoo, the tiny semi-cursive letters in Rashi script, designed as if to stymie any attempt to decipher the words. The text is tattooed across his arm exactly where the tefillin strap would go, and I wonder if Micha ever laid tefillin after he got it, and how it looked, *the leather choking the words.*

I remember that time at summer camp, when I saw Yedidia the guard just after he finished laying tefillin, and how mesmerized I was by the red marks they left on his tanned skin, but instead of touching him, I asked, "Does it hurt?"

I don't remember his answer.

Micha is staring at me with an expectant look. But what does he expect me to say?

Naama's image floats up in my mind again, blurred. This time she secretly steals Avihu's tefillin, with a particular purpose in mind. I imagine her in their small bedroom, with the lampshade that always cast a strange reddish light, picturing her slowly taking out the hidden tefillin… I wonder what they smelled like. Every tefillin set carries its owner's scent, a kind of private, clandestine, sour-bitter smell. Was that the last scent that lingered in her nostrils as she wrapped the straps around her neck? Was that what she smelled when she looked down for the last time, and saw her daughters lying supine on the floor like little dolls? *Two little dollies, one disappeared, And then there was one – just as she'd feared*… I try to blink back the flow of memories before I start wading into dangerous waters, but I can always count on Micha to drag me there anyway.

"Why were they so sure she killed herself?"

Don't look guilty. Don't look guilty. Don't look guilty.

"You don't have to look guilty," he says. "It's not like you could have stopped it."

Of course you could have. Could have and then some. I could have done things differently that last night. I wonder what's worse, the thought of Naama wrapping Avihu's sweaty tefillin straps around her neck, or the thought of someone else doing it to her.

But deep down I know there's only one possibility. I also know she was trying to tell us something, but now I'm the only one left to hear it.

"So why do you think she killed herself?" Micha elegantly ignores the look on my face and charges ahead. "Why did Naama Malchin try to murder her daughters? Why then, why that day? What happened there? Come on, Sheila, help me."

Sheila, help me. In my mind's eye, I see the trapped Jezebel lying in her cage, eyes open but unseeing, or perhaps seeing more than I can comprehend, the pups that will soon be her dinner? *The devouring mother.*

But she wasn't, poor Lilith. It was just another myth, more folklore designed to vilify, to symbolize the fear of the independent, liberated woman who does not wish to become a mother; it's not enough for them that most women already do want to become mothers, they want them *all* to want it.

But Naama didn't want to be one any more.

"Sheila, are you with me?"

Yes, but you're not with me.

"I see the possibility that Naama was murdered isn't ruffling your feathers."

Because I know it's not actually a possibility, but I have no intention of telling you that now and explaining "why then, why that day." Or what's worse, "what happened the night before the suicide." *The Night of the Long Knives.*

I lower my gaze and pick up a date cookie. It crumbles in my mouth.

"The only thing written in her file is 'post-partum depression.' Pathology was convinced it was a murder-suicide," he says.

"That makes a lot more sense," I reply. "I find it difficult to picture someone else trying to kill two babies."

"You want to tell me you find it easier to believe their own mother did that?"

Our eyes lock. I want to say yes, indeed, it's a mother's duty. *Those two belong to me!* But instead, I shove another cookie in my mouth, just to plug it.

"And that seems to you like a sufficient reason?" he asks. "Did you notice that she was depressed?"

Did I ever. We all stood by, watching Naama become thinner and thinner, wasting away, withdrawing into herself, slipping into indifference towards her sweet little twins, who gradually became as pale as their mother. Until she couldn't take it any more. *Until she took her fate into her own hands, thrump, thrump!*

My phone starts ringing and Micha glances at the name flashing on the screen. "It's Gali," he says, and I blanch inwardly. I have no intention of talking to her while Micha is sitting in front of me with that rapacious look. *Oh, Micha, what big ears you've got!*

"Well, answer her," he says.

We lock gazes for two moments, until I cave in and reach for the phone.

"Hey, Gali," I greet her with as casual a tone as I can muster.

"Hi, Sheila!" Gali's voice sounds oddly chirpy. "I wanted to ask if maybe I could interview you again for my film. I'll be a good girl, don't worry."

Well, easy for her to say, but I actually am worried, even without her sounding so very satisfied, almost unnaturally so.

"Wait, how's Jezebel?"

"Oh, Jezebel is fine now," she says with the same beaming, bubbly tone. "But I had to separate her from her babies. She started gnawing on one of their feet, and by the time I got to her, she had already swallowed it, so now he has only half a leg."

The fathers have eaten sour grapes; loving mothers boiled their own children.

The stabbing pain in my lower abdomen returns, but with Micha sitting so close, monitoring the slightest change in my expression, I make sure not a muscle in my face moves. After a few moments, he leans over and whispers something.

"What was that?" I whisper back, and he mouths, "Tell her to come over."

"Sheila, you still there?" Gali asks, and I don't know what to tell her. I've got the feeling that if she comes over, she'll be walking straight into the trap laid out for her, and that's the last thing I want. I'm already thinking how to turn down his request, but he gently places his hand on my thigh and bores deep into my eyes.

"Please," he whispers, so close I can feel his breath, "please, trust me," and he draws even closer, until his warm, muscular thigh is brushing against mine.

"Why don't you come over?" I ask, and gulp.

"I'm a bit tired," Gali replies, "I thought we'd meet tomorrow."

"Come over now, you should," I cajole, my voice cracking with betrayal. *What kind of mother are you?*

"There's someone here I'd like you to meet," I add, and Micha shoots up and takes a giant step towards the middle of the living room. Sinewy thighs indeed.

"Who?" Gali asks.

"You'll find out when you get here," I say, and feel that by mentioning a mystery guest, my act of treachery is a smidgen less treacherous. Now I just have to deal with Micha, who's looking daggers at me. But he can glare all he wants, I don't regret coming to my little munchkin's defence. *Oh, so now she's your little munchkin again?*

"Why did you tell her I'm here?" he asks, and his threatening expression fades into an insulted pout, which I'm not buying even for a second.

"I did it for you," I say with a sickly sweet tone. "So she won't feel like you tricked her and clam up."

"I would've made her open up without your help," he says, "and pardon me for saying so, but this overprotective shtick isn't becoming."

We sit silently under the Witch of Endor's gaze, and I have no doubt that if I returned the look, I'd find her expression to be one of complete content. But I don't look up.

The veil of silence has yet to lift. I remember he once told me that silence is a powerful weapon in interrogations. Very few people can bear it for long stretches, so they start blabbing away, and eventually talk themselves into jail.

I think about Naama, who was never a chatterbox, never one to trip over her tongue, *but what point is there being careful with words if you're just going to end up dangling from the ceiling?*

But the eerie glee in Gali's voice is unnerving, and it makes me wonder again what she remembers from that period. *She remembered you, didn't she.* Does she remember anything from those actual moments of horror? From the moments when her own mother turned on her?

Naama picking up a big white pillow, the red lampshade bathing the room in a blood-coloured glow.

I wonder how they took care of her afterwards, if they even sent her to a therapist or preferred to keep all the "unpleasantness" in the family. (I could swear that's what one of the relatives mumbled during the funeral, "unpleasantness" she called it, and I asked myself whether it was the aunt they brought in from the States to take care of her. I didn't dwell on it because that's exactly when Avihu noticed us out of the corner of his eye and lunged with his "Get the hell out of here.")

Only God knows how Gali turned out to be this impressive young woman, when all she had left was a screw-up like Avihu for a father. His tall, stooped figure flashes before me, with his sunken mouth, the dead look in his eyes, the stale smell of cigarettes surrounding him like a cloud. *But he wasn't always like this, something made him become like this.*

"Just an idea, but is it possible that someone went into Naama's bedroom, saw that she strangled her daughters, and then hanged her? As punishment?" I ask.

"You mean the husband?" Micha immediately replies, as if he's been waiting for that question. "Avihu Malchin was cleared of any involvement, and believe me, they looked at his alibi from every angle and it was airtight. The husband is always the first suspect."

Well, duh. The closer he is to you, the more likely to hurt you.

She came more quickly than I expected. We're sitting there, still entangled in silence, when the doorbell rings. Unlike the Grossmans' genteel wind chimes, my doorbell produces the grating blast of a train horn. *All aboard the midnight train to nowhere!*

I open the door gingerly, wanting to at least try to whisper something to her, but she walks right past me inside, a pair of long, slender legs stepping into the apartment. *Hey, girlie, what pretty legs you've got!*

She's wearing a dark, tight-fitting dress of a fabric too thick and dense for the weather we're having, and it only reinforces my suspicion that it isn't part of her everyday wardrobe. No, she wore this little number for me.

Behind me, Micha gets up, stretches out and clears his throat. "Nice to meet you," he says, "we haven't had the chance to meet until now."

Now he's staring at her, his eyes running the full length of her body: neck, chest, stomach, legs. I'd like to think of it as the usual dirty-old-man eyeing young flesh, but on second, painful thought, I realize they're too close in age, so close in fact, that if I had started early, they could both have been my children. *Yeah, right, as if this is the look a brother would fix on his sister.*

"Gali, did you forget you're coming to Bnei Brak?" I can't believe my own schoolteacherly tone. "What were you thinking with that dress?" *Shut up, you moron!*

With the two of them ogling me, I force myself to laugh, and it comes out sounding like an old witch's cackle. "It was a joke! Come on, you can't take a joke?"

No, they can't. I'm trying to catch Micha's gaze but he's avoiding me, and what's worse, Gali seems to have noticed, because all of a sudden she straightens her back and lifts her chin. *And boobs.*

"Cute place," she says, and sweeps her gaze across the living room with a look that seems more gauging and scrutinizing than it should. No, this Gali is nothing like the tiny, bleary-eyed munchkin that pressed up against me by Jezebel's cage. Nothing at all.

But why does she need to be miserable for you to love her?

I catch the flicker of hesitation in her eyes as she sits herself down in the armchair, probably because of the stains I couldn't get out, despite the very clear instructions in the various tutorials I found on YouTube. What can you expect when you get a hand-me-down living room set from a family of six? *You should be grateful!*

She glances at the cookie dish, and I say in too loud a voice, "Help yourself," even though we can both see the bowl is practically empty. But I can't bring myself to go to the kitchen and leave these two alone. *Sheila, come on, don't be one of those fairy-tale evil stepmothers, suffering from youth-envy.*

"I'll pop into the kitchen to get some more," I mumble with some effort, and head to the kitchen. I feel like I'm plodding through cement compared to Gali's nimble, gazelle-like stride, and get the sudden urge to kick her in the shins.

The new pack of cookies rips in my hand. I'm starting to sense the same heaviness I get whenever a man I'm into shows interest in another woman. This has happened to me before, more than once.

My mouth is still filled with a bitter, metallic taste when I return to the living room and place the bowl of cookies on the table. They're filled with jam. One of them has broken and the reddish filling oozed out. Obviously, that's the one Gali chooses.

"Looks like the cookie's having an abortion," she giggles, red curls bouncing, red lips parted with laughter. She picks up her phone. "This one's going straight on Insta. No filters needed."

Now they're both messing with her phone, and the quick intimacy that has sprung up between them is unmistakable. It looks so natural and easy, but I remind myself that the same kind of instant intimacy also sparked between us, even if it was quickly followed by that awful, hollow gaze he fixed on me that night when he thought I was asleep.

And now Gali is fixing her own gaze on his tattooed arm, and I wonder whether he's going to tell her about her mother and the tefillin, but he doesn't. Instead, he flexes his muscle, making the letters dance, while she gapes at him and giggles. *Giggles!*

Yes, I'll take the blubbering little orphan Gali over this simpering Sally any day.

Then I hear him say, "Someone talked me into it," and I understand he's referring to his tattoo. "Someone who could talk me into anything," he adds, and now he's giggling too.

The toddlers' teeth are set on edge.

No, this visit is not going the way it should have. I fold my hands over my stomach, feeling the swell of my flesh while staring at her impossibly thin waist, *rumour has it that certain Hollywood actresses undergo rib-removal surgery to achieve a narrower waist.* I try to understand whether there's a reason that all these emotions are suddenly roiling inside me in the middle of my living room; maybe it's another one of his interrogation techniques? After all, Micha only has two modes: good cop and better cop, *who also flirts with you, as a bonus.*

Gali finally gets up and takes her camera out of her bag. She tries to mount it on the tripod and fumbles. He rushes to her aid, of course, and their movements seem so in sync that they look like a four-armed creature (tanned, slender, young arms). I can't ignore the stealthy side glances Micha sneaks her way, and I'm starting to think he really does like her.

And when my mouth fills with that metallic taste again, my phone *GLING!*s with an incoming message.

I'm sorry. I wasn't myself. Hope you can forgive me. Neria.

Ha! The prodigal son. Obviously, this serves as an instant pick-me-up. Turns out my switch is easier to flip than I thought. All I need is to feel wanted. I read the text again and again, scouring for subtext and plot.

"So how's your dad?" I ask, a question Gali has earned fair and square.

"He's fine," she replies absent-mindedly, and adds while looking in Micha's direction, "He and Sheila don't exactly get along."

"Actually, I'd like to talk to you about that," he says.

I notice her tensing. Out of the corner of my eye, I see that Micha has noticed as well, but pretends he hasn't and starts tinkering with one of the zippers on the camera case.

"So when would be a good time to meet, just the two of us?" he asks, looking up at her.

My perked ears register the flirtatious tone, but I also pick up on something else, a subtle undertone smelling of detective's guile. While he might actually be into her, he's also no fool, this Micha.

I shift my gaze back to Gali and see just the slightest wrinkle of her nose, telling me that she too recognized and did not appreciate the undertone, and I wonder what I can say to alleviate the tension; but before I can come up with an ice-breaker, a miracle happens – the camera doesn't work! Gali tries and tries, checks the battery, presses buttons and plays with the aperture, but nothing.

Conked out.

"Let me try," Micha suggests, but she won't.

"I'll come back some other time," she says, pops the camera into its case and starts heading for the door.

I want to call out to her, Wait, you fool, don't let him see you're afraid. But I don't say a word, a decision prompted by Micha's lingering look at her long legs and shapely little behind packed in her tight dress. Joseph Pilates himself couldn't whip my arse back into that shape. Nope, it would take a dip in the fountain of youth.

"A paragon of professionalism," I can't help but blurt out the second the door closes.

"Nice of you to worry about my job," he retorts.

In lieu of answering, I get up and bend over the coffee table to start clearing the nasty dishes, *to clear everything that's nasty*, but he grabs my arm and pulls me back to the couch, next to him.

His touch is strong and intimate at the same time. I sink into the cushion.

"Say, how did Dina react to Naama's suicide?"

The question – which makes it clear that he's abandoned the theory that Naama was murdered – surprises me. I've already learned that it's better not to show him too many of my cards, so I keep a calm and composed expression. *Free of worry wrinkles.*

Obviously, there was nothing calm or composed back then. None of us could be calm, not with her suicide taking place only a day after that get-together. *The knife! Take the knife from her!* I wondered if Naama told Avihu about it. After he kicked us out of her funeral, I thought she must have told him, but I'm not so sure any more.

"Dina is the key," he says, and there's something in his tone that I can't quite put my finger on, "the first victim is always the key to solving a case, especially when it's someone like her."

"So now you're positive she was the first victim?" I want to make sure.

"A woman like Dina will always want to be the first."

Now I can put my finger on it, and I don't like it. Not one bit. I stare at the nearly empty bowls in front of me. Even the crumbs look gross.

"From what I understand she was the dominant figure in every area of her life, even in the Others, even the decision to not have kids."

"We made that decision together," I say. "It's what we all wanted. It worked for us."

"Is it still working?" he asks very quietly.

"It's something that sinks in and sets," I reply, surprising even myself. "It forms inside you slowly, and then you realize it's where your life is heading, even if there are questions and doubts along the way."

I fall silent, realizing I said more than I wanted to, but it's the truth. With or without Dina, the choice of a childless life is something that settles and congeals very slowly, maybe too slowly, along with other life choices. And what was right for us during our youth, for the women we were back then, isn't necessarily right for us in our adult life.

Because what we wanted back in college was one thing and one thing only: to make sure we didn't become like everyone else, didn't veer down the popular path of snagging a prince and popping out babies and accidentally falling asleep for a thousand years. The Others was our act of defiance against this path. Today I realize it was a pretty juvenile gesture. Today I can also understand that the "everyone else" that used to terrify us isn't so bad; it's just not for me, and not necessarily out of defiance but out of a deep, visceral knowledge.

I look at Micha with what I hope passes as indifference. If only he knew what his question sparked in me, *or maybe he does know and that's exactly why he asked.*

My gaze drifts across the armchairs, stained with the marks of other people's children. No matter how hard I scrubbed the upholstery, the stains wouldn't budge; they're still here, as if celebrating a private victory. *But over who?*

"You sound less decisive than usual," Micha says, and I see a hint of a smile. "What would Dina say?"

Again with Dina?

"I don't know, she's dead," I say, and head to the toilet, only to discover the first bloodstain, dark and curdled like all first stains, and I stare at it and then reach down and touch my pants, worrying the fabric, waiting for the sweet wave of relief to wash over me, and it indeed arrives, but not as quickly as I thought it would, not at all.

I stay there, sitting on the toilet, counting the floor tiles in front of me over and over again like a record stuck in a groove, until I hear Micha calling out from the living room asking if everything's okay, and I shout back, Yeah, sure, of course, everything's fine, fine, fine, fine, fine.

Just fine.

21

DINA'S SPRAWLED OUT on the grass, her hair spilling over her face like a veil. To the innocent onlooker she probably looks calm and at peace, but I can see how tense she is. *She wants to catch you.*

This memory is alive and vivid. Funny how I've forgotten everything I learned inside the classrooms of Bar-Ilan University ages ago, but everything I learned outside the classroom is still as fresh as if it happened this morning.

In that memory, Ronit and Naama are also splayed on the grass, surrounded by open notebooks, the air rich with the warm and sweet end-of-spring scent. Maybe I knew while it was happening that that's how I wanted to remember us, a bunch of students lazing on the grass under a soft sun. I think there was even a butterfly fluttering around us, landing on the tip of Dina's nose, but I have to say I've begun to doubt the accuracy of this memory.

"Having a kid is supposed to be a guarantee that you'll leave something behind," Dina says, with a semi-sleepy voice that doesn't fool me for a minute. "That a part of you will live on, that you'll be remembered."

"It's not completely far-fetched," I reply, and hear Ronit giggling behind me (maybe the butterfly landed on her nose?).

"What's your mum's name?" Dina asks, and the question takes me by surprise.

"Sarah."

"And her mum?"

"Bella."

"And her mum?" Dina's voice has lost its feigned drowsiness, and I recognize that subtle quality creeping into it.

"Sheila!" I call out triumphantly, "You didn't think I'd know, did you?"

"Honestly, I'm surprised you know," she admits, "but that's only because you're a narcissist. If you weren't named after her, there's no way you'd know your great-grandmother's name."

Ronit is giggling behind me again, but this time I know it's not because of the butterfly. Dina props herself up on her elbows, the curtains of her dark straight hair parting to reveal her fair skin. She looks like an Inuit with a pair of bulging black spotlights for eyes.

"I'm willing to bet neither of you know the names of your great-grandmothers," she says to Ronit and Naama. "I actually conducted a little survey here on campus, and almost no one knows, or even cares to know. And yet everyone's so worried about leaving something behind, living on in people's memories..."

Dina scoffs. Ronit and I join her, and all our snickering soon turns into hysterical giggles. I remember that laughing fit on the grass, and I remember the butterfly, yes, there was a butterfly there, I'm sure of it now, and the three of us laughed and laughed until our sides hurt.

It's a shame that by then Naama wasn't laughing along with us.

The bead eyes of the wax figurines are glimmering in front of me. "You came back to us," they're saying, "and this time it's for good." When Efraim called to ask me to come back to work, I had no idea how happy I'd be to see them again, and now I realize I missed them a lot more than I missed my colleagues.

And here they are before me, my dear old friends, shiny and polished of dust (maybe I could book the museum cleaners for a one-off emergency gig at my place?). I move slowly from one figurine to the next, until I reach Michal's.

The crown is perched on her head more crookedly than usual. I straighten it and study her beautiful, sad face. I think I'm starting to understand the reason for her sadness, and it has nothing to do with her not having kids, and everything to do with the dude she married, because that's what happens when a princess marries a shepherd. Especially when her deepest desires – even those she isn't aware of – aren't compatible with his. Compatibility is everything.

Almost despite myself, I think about Micha, *What's the matter with you? Whatever you two had it was over before it started*, and I also think about Maor, and about how they're both twenty-six, they're always twenty-six, frozen in time while I keep getting older.

I peer into Michal's morose eyes and realize that if I'm not careful, I might end up like a frozen wax figurine, a dried-up old hag coated in epoxy for posterity. *Even the lonely, desperate boys won't want you.*

Something inside me snaps. I whip a pen out of my bag and start doodling tefillin straps on Michal's left arm. It's a razor-point Pilot pen and I'm carving the black lines into her wax skin when one of the security guards decides this is a good time to see what's going on at the other end of the pavilion (my end), so I skedaddle before I get to see whether Michal's eyes are less gloomy now.

Efraim is all smiles when he greets me at the entrance to the auditorium.

When Eli called to say Efraim "absolutely can't wait" to have me back at the museum, I found it hard to believe, but there he is, quivering and jubilant as a groom under the chuppah.

"Ah, the prodigal daughter!" he trumpets, and Shirley rolls her eyes behind his back. Sometimes I envy Efraim for his oafish tactlessness. Makes life a lot easier.

Shirley looks different, a kind of squished, more haggard version of herself, and I wonder if she's made any progress with the sperm bank, or maybe even had the insemination, but I don't smell any traces of hormones or new life.

Before I take a step towards her, Efraim pulls me aside.

"Guess what," he says, even his beard bouncing with excitement.

"What."

"'Bible, Books and Beyond'! They want you!"

For a fleeting moment, I feel the pinprick of excitement. "Bible, Books and Beyond" is the most prestigious of all national Bible conferences, the holy grail for Bible lecturers – an annual, three-day event packed with lectures, concerts and various "attractions." I always turned my nose up at the conference for being "commercialized to the point of charging admission." Deep down I knew though the real reason was that I'd never been invited to take part, and I'd already given up any hope of ever being invited, but here it is, the moment has come.

"What do they want me to talk about?" I ask, but mid-question I realize what the answer's going to be.

"The childfree women of the Bible, of course," Efraim informs me with that harmless-uncle tone of his, but behind the thick lenses of his glasses, his eyes narrow, gearing up for war.

"And this lecture needs to be ready when exactly?"

"It's not just a lecture, it's going to be with live music, a finalist from last season's 'Israeli Idol,' that girl with the short hair!"

"When?" I repeat the question.

"Next week."

"Wow, do they always organize their impressive conferences so quickly?" I play dumb, but Efraim is smart enough not to answer, and lets me finish, "Or am I a last-minute substitute for a lecture they actually scheduled long ago?"

I ask that last question so loudly that a few heads turn in our direction. *They know.*

"Well, of course you're standing in for someone," Efraim replies, "and it's a terrific opportunity for you!"

"And for the museum," I add. "So who am I standing in for?"

Who do you think?

"Dina Kaminer," he replies plainly, smiling as if that's the best thing about the invitation, and then, without missing a beat or batting an eye, he adds, "And I already told them you'd do it." Once again, I see the advantage of his emotional obliviousness, how easy his life must be.

"Excuse me?"

"Sheila, you have to do it. It could really bump you up the ladder!"

I start mumbling something about how it doesn't feel right, *and Dina!*, and that it would be insensitive, and what would everyone say, *and Dina!*, and how could I even consider such a thing, *and Dina!*, and when he takes a step closer and grabs my hand, I feel his fingernails digging into my skin.

"This is a golden opportunity for you," he whispers and leans even closer, his face inches from mine, "and I won't let you pass on it, *capisce*?"

How did you become such a loser?

"I know you've been waiting a long time for this opportunity, so here is, it finally came; now don't let it slip by!" The subtext assails my ears: don't let this slip by *as well*, loser.

He finally releases me from his clasp, but the fingernail marks will stay with me for the rest of the day.

The commotion on the other side of the door lets me know my group has arrived.

Efraim smiles at me. "See? You got a special group, so you won't let all the fame go to your head."

I want to tell him just where he can shove all that fame, but I hear the sound of a chair being thrown and a panicked scream outside, and I take a deep breath and steel myself for a bumpy ride.

Because "special" is our euphemism for any group whose members meet the definition of challenged – from the ADHD kids to the developmentally handicapped.

I usually enjoy being their instructor. They don't try to impress anyone with wisecracks and stale witticisms, they don't usually demand anything of me and the instruction usually amounts to a few short educational videos and a quick stroll through the wax pavilion. But it does require an extra security guard in the pavilion, because the kids usually ignore our warnings and touch, poke and pinch the figurines. I always get the feeling that the figurines tense up whenever a "special" group arrives, apart from our mother Leah, who just gives them her patient, hollow look.

I venture into the foyer armed with my most professional smile, and who do I see there, standing by a loud group of kids and their chaperoning special ed assistant? The queen of make-up don'ts, Taliunger, her face plied with cakey foundation, blinking with a surprise that matches my own. *That's what you think.*

"Tali! What a surprise!" I drag out the words.

"Yes, yes, it certainly is," she blurts but quickly pulls herself together, "so this is your kingdom?"

And she holds her hand out with that sweeping gesture as if she's in her private living room, the tiny empress's magisterial wave, painted fingernails sparkling. *But this time I'm the empress.*

I wave the assistant over and together we start seating the children in front of the screen. Some of them sit down obediently while others refuse and burst into loud squeals of protest. I wonder why Taliunger came with them, and as if reading my mind, she says, "I'm just filling in for one of the instructors, only for today. I'm a counsellor, not some instructor."

My comeback is an uncontrollable outburst, "I'm starring at next week's Bible conference, it's going to be me and a super-famous singer. I'm not at liberty to say who yet, but let's just say jaws are going to drop. Should I get you and Neria tickets?"

Her tiny body tenses, and I wonder if it's because of the mystery musician or the way I dragged out that *Neria*, as if savouring the name on my tongue.

I sweep my eyes over the kids to make sure they're all sitting comfortably for the opening movie, and my gaze lingers on a girl who, for some reason, is still standing. She's an itty-bitty thing, sweet and owlish, with pigtails and glasses with lenses like bottle bottoms. I gently help her to sit, and she extends a tiny finger and shows me a fresh scratch. "Meir did that to me," she purrs. Her speech is garbled and she repeats the sentence several times until I manage to parse the words.

"That's not nice of him at all!" I say, and she smiles at me, flashing Bazooka pink gums. I can't make out how old she is. Seven? Eight? She looks like an underbaked baby, and her bird-like features and sugary smile tug at my heart.

The lights are switched off and the movie begins. We always choose the same video for "special" groups, "The Fathers and the Mothers." It's a cartoon musical, not exactly thought-provoking, but it does the job. Nine times out of ten, it keeps the kids quiet and glued to the screen.

Tali and I lean against the wall at the far end of the dark room. To anyone looking from the outside, we probably seem like two chummy instructors, *but no one's looking.* We're both staring at the screen without blinking, inhaling and exhaling the same sour air, while in the video, our mother Sarah starts torturing Hagar. The animator chose to draw Sarah as a ghoulish hag with hook nose. *A childless shrew.* It's only after she has Yitzhak that the animator will magically smooth out her wrinkles and she'll go back to being the pleasant, loving woman she once was.

Taliunger leans closer to me.

"I'd appreciate it if you backed off Neria," she says.

"What?" It takes me a moment to understand what she said, as if the words were in a foreign language.

"You heard me. And don't come over to our house again," she replies, emphasizing the *our.*

With vindictive relish, I recall Neria's text. It took me some time to answer, and after quite a few carefully worded messages which I deleted, restored and deleted again, I sent: *We're cool, Neria.*

A simple, elegant answer. We're good. From my experience, the more stoic you pretend to be, the harder they chase you, so my reply wasn't exactly driven by benevolence, *and no, we're not cool, Neria.*

"Better focus on your *glamorous* job," Taliunger whispers to me, so close I can feel her greasy make-up smudging my ear, "since, really, that's the only thing you've got."

Her straightforwardness surprises me. This is not how I remembered her. Dina was the straight shooter among us, and Taliunger a stealthier, back-stabbing type. But I guess motherhood forces you to look life in the face, and not waste time with detours.

To tell you the truth, it's one of the things that always scared me, the changes your kids force on you, changes of the most profound kind, far-reaching kind, drastic changes in your behaviour and attitude.

What can I tell you? Even if you're not that great, it doesn't mean you're willing to change.

Still with our backs to the wall, we're staring straight ahead as Abraham banishes Hagar to the desert, *see? He's willing to sacrifice his other son too.*

"Just for the record, my job is just as glamorous as yours," I whisper to Taliunger, "and the invite to the conference still stands."

"Unfortunately, it's right when I'm putting the kids to sleep," she replies.

A part of me is slightly disappointed with her answer, *That's your comeback, really? The kids' bedtime?*

I look at the weary, aching Sarah, and even though I've seen this movie dozens of times, my heart sinks. Because no matter how full her life is, so much living and doing alongside her husband, it's not enough for her, and for the first time, I can't help but wonder whether all my living and doing is enough for me.

The note with the "Israeli Idol" finalist is pulsing in my hand. *Thrump! Thrump!*

Thank God, the movie's over. I can't bear to stand next to Taliunger even one more minute, and the feeling seems to be mutual, because once the lights are flicked back on, we each dart to opposite ends of the auditorium.

Now we're walking the kids in single (and crooked) file to the wax pavilion, and I wave the extra guard over to join us. I feel like I'm on autopilot, reciting the safety procedures, lecturing about the figurines, saying all the right words but with a heavy, cloudy mind.

Suddenly I hear the guard shouting, "What did you do?" with unbridled aggression.

I rush across the auditorium, in the direction of the Michal figure, who's sitting there with her frozen gaze, my "tefillin" burning into her arm, and next to her stands the sweet, pigtailed owl holding a pen, her tiny body shaking.

"I just drew a flower next to the scratch," she stutters and extends her arm innocently, showing me the tiny flower doodled next to her red scratch. Unfortunately, she drew it with the same pen I used to scribble the tefillin on Michal.

"Tamara!" Despite her petite size, Taliunger seems to tower over the owl like a gloomy presence. "What did you do?! Bad girl! Bad!"

And you're a bad, bad counsellor, I want to say but don't, and just when I'm about to intervene, the special ed assistant appears with the chief security guard, an older man with a raging red face, and they're all closing in on Tamara, who's curling into herself, trembling and blubbering, "No... I didn't... not me..."

"Don't lie, Tamara!"

Taliunger is much angrier than is warranted by such a minor event, *Where's all this anger coming from? How old is this anger?* But unfortunately, she's not the only one – they're all glowering at Tamara with daunting disapproval, and my heart goes out to the little girl whose pigtails are fluttering with fear, but I can't utter a single word.

Well, speak up!

I can't do it.

Speak up!

I can't.

Speak!

Can't.

Even Michal is staring at me with her cold eyes, *What are you waiting for? Go on! Help your little girl!*

But that's just it. Tamara *isn't* my little girl. I have no doubt that if she were, I'd find it in me to confess, right away, without blinking. Because that's what your kids make you do; they make you forget about yourself, about your habits, your fears, the many moments of shame and avoidance that have shaped you into who you are. Your kids will make you stretch the limits of your selflessness beyond recognition.

And *that* I just can't do. Can't.

Gloom lingers like a fog over the house.

I spend the entire evening sitting and staring at the walls, feeling depleted. The note with the "Idol" finalist's phone number is neatly folded in my hand, but I can't move, let alone speak. Tamara's tiny, insulted owlish face is floating before me. *Who wants a hug? Who wants a cuddle?*

I'm still wall-watching when my phone bleeps with an incoming message. It's a picture sent from an unknown caller, and I zoom in and see a blue, contorted face. A few moment pass until I realize it's a picture of a drowned witch, with weights tied to her ankles and a rope coiled around her entire body, only her hair loose, unspooling like ribbons in the water. Her dead eyes are looking straight at me. It's me.

22

NO, IT'S NOT ME, CAN'T BE.

Of course not, you were never a real witch, no matter how hard you tried.

I hold the phone up and eye the picture. It's a painting. Whoever sent it obviously put in some serious effort. The resemblance is there, mostly around the jawline, and the thin hair floating around. Maybe something in the shape of our mouths. But the face in the painting is bloated and ugly. *The face of a witch who failed the test.*

With a detachment that surprises me, I continue to study the painting. It's clearly a scene depicting the infamous "swimming test" from the Middle Ages, and even though I can't determine the exact period, there's something familiar about it; it rings a muffled but important bell, *remember!* But I can't.

The swimming test was simple and cruel: if you were charged with witchcraft, you were bound with ropes, walked to the nearest river and tossed in.

If you somehow managed not to drown, well then, you're a witch destined to burn at the stake. But if you sank like a stone? It's a shame, of course, but at least it proves you're not guilty.

And what about you, Sheila, guilty or innocent?

I stay up all night, my phone burning in my hand like a lump of coal. I study the painting from every angle, this presumably being the first contact the killer has made with me, and I feel like

I'm whispering an old incantation. The painting is threatening and mocking me at the same time, it was sent to remind me of something, something from *ages ago*… but what?

I mull over the entire chain of events, picking it apart from the moment it all began, from the moment Dina was murdered and things started spiralling. But was Dina's murder really the beginning? *Think, woman! Was it ground zero?* Is it possible that this thing started long before that? Maybe, say, when four young women met on the grassy mound behind the campus cafeteria, long, long ago?

Hercule Poirot always said you have to look for the starting point – there's one moment when it all began, and once you identify it, you're halfway there. That's all very nice, Hercule, but what is that moment?

Deep down, you already know.

The drowned witch is flashing me her eternal, submerged smile, and something flickers and flutters at the edge of my consciousness, a niggling memory, fighting to reach the surface. It has something to do with Dina, I know it, something that was said, *or wasn't said*, during that last visit. That something is right there, waiting, lurking.

Go back to the starting point, the moment it all began, Poirot's words echo in my mind all night. He never had kids, nor did Miss Marple; their lives were more than full without them. Maybe that's the reason they became detectives, *not to leave your own traces, but to track the traces left by someone else.*

I'm sitting in my living room, staring at the painting, the dead witch silently staring back at me as the minutes turn into hours.

Tick-tock, tick-tock, tick-tock.

*

Micha's reaction comes as a surprise, and not a pleasant one.

Oh, come on, when has he ever pleasantly surprised you? It's been a few days since we last met, a few days in which he hasn't contacted me, and the look he gives me when I show him the picture is the condescending amusement of a man who was waiting for this moment, *a look that says, I knew she'd find some cockamamie excuse to see me again, this is the best she could come up with?*

He asks a bunch of questions with that half-mocking gaze and offhanded tone, and slowly but surely it sinks in: no, he doesn't believe me.

"You're acting as if I sent that photo to myself." I can't hold back.

"I didn't say that."

You don't need to, your tone is doing it for you.

"So why aren't you rushing to find out who sent it?"

"It's not that simple. We'd need to get a court order for the phone company, and then have people assigned to it, and our security department is pretty much two cops. You see, this isn't high up on the priority list, so it'll take them time to—"

"Then explain to them how urgent this is, and they'll make it a priority."

He keeps his eyes on his phone while I'm talking, inert but for his thumb sliding across the screen, a model of indifference. I'm trying to understand what caused this shift, we were so intimate, we were almost… flashes of me sitting on the toilet, dripping red, float before me; for an hour and a half I was almost… we were almost… maybe in some subconscious way he sensed the threat and his instincts screamed, *run, man, run!*

Sitting on the edge of the couch with his gaze still on his phone, he doesn't bother to hide his boredom.

I look down at my own phone and see the drowned witch looking back at me with a sympathetic smile, and I wonder why I'm not afraid of her, wasn't afraid of her even for a moment, when this picture is supposed to be an explicit threat.

No threats, girlfriend, I'm your sister-in-arms! Now get this man on your couch off his arse.

I nip into the kitchen and return with a meat cleaver. Unused, it's spotless and shiny. For a moment his eyes grow wide with panic, and that moment is all I needed. He doesn't trust me, never did.

"I want you to teach me how to defend myself in case the murderer shows up here," I say, trying to imbue my voice with genuine distress.

"Sheila, you don't actually think someone's going to show up." Again with that dismissive tone of his.

"You piece of shit," my voice nearly booms, "what gives you the right to be so blasé about this?"

What gives you the right to be so blasé about me?

He gets up, lunges at me and snatches the knife with zero effort, just plucks it from my fingers like a ripe piece of fruit. Turns out whatever sexual power he had over me is still there, but that's *all he has.*

"You shouldn't play with knives," he says, "because if someone *does* come after you, he'll just use it against you."

"Then teach me how to use it."

"There's not much to teach," he replies.

"Don't you remember how in *Face/Off,* John Travolta teaches his daughter how to stab her boyfriend in the thigh and twist the knife so the wound won't close?" Almost involuntarily, I recall our first conversation with all the flirty banter, and for a moment I think I can see a tiny sparkle in his eyes; but it's just my imagination, because the next thing I know he's glancing at his watch and "suddenly remembers" he has to go. Obviously, he'll update me about any new developments, *if* there are any.

Poof! Micha's gone.

Only after the door shuts behind him, I remember that the father in the movie, the one who taught his daughter how to twist the knife, wasn't even her real father – it was the impostor.

That's life. You never get the useful information from the people closest to you.

With Gali's face inches from mine, I can see the blonde peach fuzz on her upper lip. *Does she bleach it, or is it naturally fair like it usually is with redheads?* I take a step back.

"But I'm going to need a close-up of you later," she says, while fiddling with the tripod. She's going on and on about her poor camera and everything that's wrong with it and how long it took her to find a decent repair shop and how the technician reminded her of a neighbour they once had. She's rambling so badly that I know beyond a shadow of a doubt that there was nothing wrong with the camera, not even for a moment.

"You seem kind of down," she offers gently, and I, sick of all the pretending, decide to tell her why.

"Can you show me the picture?" The eagerness in her voice – snuffing out any trace of its former gentleness – makes me flinch, but it's too late to back out. "I absolutely love witches," she adds.

Yes, they all love them when they're young.

I study her while her eyes devour the picture, and once again I get that niggling feeling that I know this witch, that I've seen her before. *Remember!*

"Micha isn't helping you find out who sent it?" She utters his name so casually, but it doesn't bother me any more. I mean, it almost doesn't.

"No, not really."

"Well, he's kind of a douchebag," she says. "I hope you know that."

I consider her as she tinkers with the aperture, but there's something flickering behind that quiet tone, and when she looks up and our eyes meet, pupil to pupil, I realize that I do know that. Micha is a douchebag.

"Can I make coffee?" She hasn't finished asking and already she's on her way to the kitchen. I'm surprised to find that I feel rather comfortable with it, that I don't mind her seeing the stained floor and the sticky mess on the counter, the grimy dishes lying in the sink. *Two little dollies, taking it on the chin… two little dollies, comfortable in their own skin.*

I hear her opening the high cupboard, and know which mugs she's going to choose. The pretty special-occasion mugs I never (ever) use. They're white bone china with a thin gold trim that means you should never put them in the microwave, unless you want them to explode. *Let them explode! Let it all explode!*

When she hands me a mug, I feel the heat permeating my palms and recall an article I read about how men who were served a cup of hot coffee by a pretty woman would rate her more attractive than the men to whom she served a cold cup.

No surprises there, huh? Warmth, nourishment, love, home, they all speak the same language, all of them, always. *Let them explode! Let it all explode!*

Above the mug's gilded rim, Gali's face looks soft and flushed. The rosy cheeks lend her a childish vulnerability, but something about the slow, measured way she stirs her spoon keeps me from taking a sip. Her small hand swirls the spoon clockwise, then counter-clockwise, while my own hands clutching my mug are still and sweaty, the gilded edge glistening menacingly.

"Where did you come from all of a sudden?" My teeth clink against the china, and I wonder whether they'll scratch the enamel.

"What do you mean?" While there's genuine surprise in her voice, I get the feeling she knows perfectly well what I mean.

"You know that in books, when someone suddenly appears after a wave of murders, that person's usually the murderer."

I can't believe those words just came out of my mouth, words I didn't believe I could think, *What's going on with you? This is your little munchkin!*

But this grown-up munchkin in front of me isn't flinching. "I came precisely because of the murders," she says. "Once Dina was killed, I realized I had to make this video now, because who knows what's going to happen." Her voice trails off. We both know what's going to happen.

"What do you remember about my mum?" Her voice suddenly sounds childish, but then again, everyone sounds like a child when they say "my mum." *That's just how it is, you never stop being mummy's baby.*

What can I possibly tell her? I hang my head low, and my eyes land on the painting of the dead witch, and all at once, it hits me.

Frida Gotteskind's Witches throughout History course! The four of us took that course together first semester, and the lecturer was a fat and chipper Belgian who got divorced two months into the course, and then wasn't so chipper or chubby any more. In fact, she lost so much weight she went from chubby to scrawny and sunken, and ended up looking, well, not unlike a witch.

She used to show us slides of witches who had been tortured and dragged and burned and drowned, and those drawings looked a lot like this one, with the same elusive, dreamlike quality.

This is it, Sheila, the past has come knocking. It'll always haunt you, even if you thought you left it all behind. Got that, Witchiepoo?

I eye Gali. If the person who sent me the picture was in Frida Gotteskind's course, it couldn't have been her. *Think! Remember!*

I'm so caught up in my thoughts that Gali has to repeat the question, and unfortunately, I blurt out the first thing that pops into my mind.

"I guess my most vivid memory of Naama is from that last night."

Stupid, stupid woman! Why do you always have to open your big mouth? Gali baulks and backs into the tripod, and the camera crashes to the floor with a loud thud. There's a strange, faint cracking sound, followed by a series of tiny crackles. *Clink! Clang! Crack! Thrump! Thrump! Thrump!*

Okay, this time the camera is unmistakably broken. Gali looks like a little girl standing in the middle of the living room after breaking a bowl of candy, just standing there with her knees shaking, blinking into the light.

"What happened then, Sheila?" she asks with the same babyish voice. "What really happened that night? I want to know."

And even though I want to tell her, *yearn to tell her!*, I know the moment I do, she'll turn against me and hate me forever, because with all due respect to special relationships and the whole "friends are the family we choose" modern hogwash, friends *are not* family, and friends of your mother's are certainly not family – only your family is family, only your family is forever, and if for some reason you choose not to have one, there's a good chance you'll end up alone. *Got that, Witchiepoo?*

Gali's eyes bore into my face, and her expression turns icy.

"I understand you're not going to tell me," she says.

"Not yet."

"Then when? When it's too late?" Her words linger in the air.

Don't you get it? It's already too late.

"I have a friend who knows someone in the Mossad; he can probably help you with the picture," she says, her voice surprisingly stringent. "I'll help you, but just remember that you won't help me."

She bends over and starts picking up the camera pieces. She does this slowly, shard after shard, like a little girl trying to put a broken doll back together, then turns and leaves without looking back or saying goodbye.

Sitting at the computer, I'm focusing so hard on googling the painting, *who knew there were so many dead witches under the water?*, that I don't hear my phone ringing, and only upon the caller's second attempt, do I notice it and answer impatiently.

It takes some time to realize that the blurry, bizarre déjà vu is from the gravelly, matter-of-fact female voice asking my name and requesting I come to the police station – exactly the voice I imagined hearing before that first phone call from Micha.

"When do you want me to come?" I ask.

"Tomorrow morning."

"Then why didn't Micha say anything to me? I already saw him today." While the words pour out of me, I wonder whether the reason Micha didn't say anything is because he is no longer on my side, and maybe never was.

"Who?" the gravelly voice asks, bewildered.

"Micha, Micha—" It takes me a moment to recall his last name, and the dense silence on the end of the line doesn't help. "Yarden. Micha Yarden."

"Amiram Yarden?" she asks.

"No. Micha, your detective," I reply. Very slowly.

"I have no idea who you're talking about."

The words reach me as if through thick fog, and not as a poetic expression of mystery, but actual fog, the kind that fills your skull and chest and makes it hard to breathe.

I sit down in my stained armchair, and from within this fog that continues to billow inside me, I hear the gravelly voice repeat and insist, "I don't know who you're talking about, we don't have a detective named Micha Yarden here."

She repeats it one last time, and this time her voice is tinted with sorrow, as if apologizing for being the bearer of this answer.

23

THE PERSON LOOKING BACK at me in the mirror at the police station is pale and dishevelled. *The village fool! The village idiot!*

The police officer sent to escort me is regarding me with a suspicious leer, but I can't pull myself away from the mirror. The face reflected in it is that of a magic-less witch. *Little witch, little witch cheated and tricked!*

"Shall we?" the officer asks, her tiny mouth working a piece of gum. "They're waiting for us upstairs."

But I can't move. On each side of the mirror stands a large glass cabinet crammed with golden trophies. I wonder how and why they were awarded all these trophies, for all the mounting corpses? For impersonation?

Since that phone call I've been walking inside a thick cloud, a thousand drowned witches floating inside me, a thousand questions screaming in my head. Who is he? Who is he? Who is this man? *Who's this baby? Who?*

Dina's voice is panting in my ear, *I told you you're an idiot*, a vindicated voice, but there's something else lurking inside it, something I should have recognized a long time ago.

Micha's face flits before me, a face that has undergone multiple changes in a surprisingly short period of time: the boyish, trusting face, dimple appearing through delicate stubble; the face of the man who leaned in for a kiss; the indifferent, uncaring face from our last meeting; and hovering above those faces, the one that stared at me at night. A stony face with empty eyes.

But he knew! Knew everything, every detail of the investigation, *don't think about it!*, he knew about events that were to take place, even knew about Debby and Saul, knew what no one could have known unless he was a police detective, but maybe... *don't think about it!*

For one wild moment I wonder whether I imagined it all, whether Micha was just a figment of my imagination, someone who existed only within the walls of my apartment, *and your bedroom.* This is what it feels like when the rug is pulled out from under you. A river is running below me, and my pockets are heavy with rocks.

You failed the test. Next witch! And she better not be a sucker like you!

I shuffle down the narrow corridor with the bubblegum-smacking officer bouncing behind me, talking on the phone in a high-pitched squeak. She definitely isn't the gravel-voiced cop who called me. *I have no idea who you're talking about. Who is he? Who? Beware of that man-child, that's exactly the type who ends up taking a chainsaw to their mummy.*

I remember that look, a scrutinizing, waiting-in-the-shadows look, a look that shouldn't have been there. But was it the look of a killer? *Come on, Sheila, don't give that baby so much credit.* Micha the killer? The thought almost makes me smile. It's so ridiculous it never even crossed my mind, not even during that long, black night that went on and on and that felt like it was never going to end. *Not him!* Because let's face it, he doesn't have it in him, doesn't have a sliver of what it takes. Never did. He's too boring to be the killer. Maor, Micha. They were really quite similar in the end.

The narrow corridor widens and I can hear the echo of my footsteps; and not for the first time since this all began, I wonder why I'm not afraid. How could it be that throughout this whole episode, I never felt as scared as I should?

Because you're smart, that's why. You always were.

It's Dina again, but this time the voice is encouraging, almost seductive. I know she's right. It's time I go back to being smart.

Unlike during our last encounter, this time Debby seems nicer, and not as short. She's sitting behind a giant computer in a small room with bare walls. I remember having read somewhere that investigation rooms are never decorated with anything that might distract the suspect. *Emptiness as a solution.*

"Coffee?" Debby offers, looking at me almost affectionately, and I wonder why. None of the possibilities I can think of is encouraging.

"Yes, please," I say, hoping I'll be able to swallow and keep it down. I haven't had even a tiny sip of anything since yesterday. *Trap's finally shut.*

"By the way, who's that Micha you asked about?" Debby casually enquires, and I freeze.

"Just a guy. Friend on the force," I say with a voice that even I can tell sounds strained and unnatural, and I think of Neria Grossman. *I have a friend on the police force.*

Debby looks at me, narrowing her eyes with scrutiny. Too much scrutiny. "Jeez, you look awful," she says, somehow suffusing the words with genuine concern. "Are you sure you feel well enough to help us?"

"So you took me off your suspect list?" *God, Sheila, now you decide to open your trap?*

"You?" she asks, with a look I can't read. "You were never on it. We had your ER discharge letter."

Now I can make out the look. She's telling me the truth. I'd gotten so used to Micha's lies and bullying that I forgot what the truth looks like. *You silly goose!*

"We wanted to show you something interesting we found on Dina Kaminer's computer," Debby says, and I try to listen. To listen very carefully. "Maybe you could give us more information, shed some light on this."

At first I wonder whether they're going to show me another picture of Frida Gotteskind's drowned witches, but when Debby turns the computer screen in my direction, there's no picture, only words.

"We found this in her Gmail drafts," she says. "Dina wrote it shortly after you left her apartment. She probably meant to send it to you but didn't make it."

No, she didn't make it. But I recall everything she did manage to do, including at our last meeting, and alongside the usual bitterness and rage that bubble to the surface is another, unidentified feeling in the mix. *Focus! Focus!*

I feel Debby's pinprick eyes resting on me, but her gaze isn't piercing; it's soft when she says, "And I feel I should tell you before you read the letter, that Dina Kaminer was pregnant."

Dina was pregnant. Dina was pregnant. Dina was pregnant. No, the words don't go together.

I stare at Debby, who doesn't take her eyes off me. Dina was pregnant. Dina was pregnant. *The young Dina, sprawled on the grass, her voice humming the familiar tune, "No one wants kids, and no one needs kids, and we'll never ever have them, n-e-v-e-r!"*

But apparently she did want one, need one, she, of all women. Or maybe it shouldn't have come as such a surprise? Maybe the thing that scares you most is the thing you secretly crave? Maybe it was the same tenacious vitality that always drove her forward, the forceful energy that pushed her to get up and take action, that eventually made her yearn for a child of her own?

It always ends with a baby, you'll all want one, just wait and see.

Some biblical exegeses claim that even Miriam the prophetess ended up getting married and having three kids, and I always wondered whether the rabbis behind this interpretation couldn't bear that such a powerful prophetess chose not to have babies, or just felt bad for the woman and decided to bestow upon her the sacred gift of childbirth.

I expect the room to start spinning around me, but the naked walls are steady and still, *Dina was pregnant.* Everything sharpens and crystallizes like icicles, and all at once I realize just what has bugged me all along, what chafed at the edge of my consciousness at night before falling asleep, like an incessant itch.

Because I knew, I did. I knew it the moment she opened the door, her face bloated with that subtle hormonal fullness, that rosy glow, the distinct scent of pregnancy that I could always sniff out on a woman, even from the way she walked and sat down. She was *carrying.* And I almost knew it.

There, now you know.

I can't read the email, the letters are dancing on the screen. *Dina was pregnant.* But I feel Debby's expectant gaze on me, and force myself to blink and focus on the very short text.

Dear Sheila,

You left my house in anger, and I'm very sorry for that. It's not what I wanted. Quite the opposite. There was a happy reason behind my invitation, and I wanted to clear the air between us, to mend years of wrongdoing.

You see, this is a period of renewal and great change for me, I—

I raise my eyes from the screen and meet Debby's pointed look. For some reason she doesn't seem as nice now.

"According to our timeline, she stopped writing to open the door for the killer."

I feel a stabbing pain when I imagine Dina bent over her keyboard, writing her reconciling words. I more than anyone know how hard it was for her to apologize, she never owned her mistakes, no matter what price she had to pay. "Only losers apologize, or stupid women," she used to say with that famous determination of hers, but here it is, this apology, *this pregnancy.* Dina is the proof that people can change.

Who knows, maybe you can too, one day.

"We're assuming that with her pregnancy, Dina decided to reach out to more people from her past, and it very well may be that one of them is our murderer." Debby takes a noisy sip from a giant cup of coffee that I only now notice, and says, "So we want to go over the list of people you and Dina both knew again."

She takes another slurpy sip and gives me a conspiratorial look. I feel like telling her, "Oh, so now we're best friends?" but I don't have time for that. There's someone on the list of "people you and Dina both knew," *knew very well indeed!* that I'm going to see the moment they let me leave this place.

24

THE UGLY GREEN ceramic sign on his door announces: Yarden.

For a moment I feel a surge of relief. At least that's his real name, at least that wasn't a lie. *At least he's not a figment of your imagination.*

Thrump, thrump! Thrump, thrump! I knock as hard as I can, pounding with balled fists. *Thrump, thrump!* My hands are starting to hurt, but I'm not giving up, I know he's in there.

"Open up! Open the door, you piece of shit!" I shout, "Open the door, arsehole!"

When my shouts become too loud (had I known how liberating it is to scream at the top of your lungs, I would have started shouting a long time ago), the door opens abruptly, and he pulls me inside.

Once my eyes adjust to the blinding neon light, we stare at each other silently. He's wearing an old, loose-for-wear wife beater, looking grubbier than usual, his stubble darker than usual and eyes lighter than usual – their gaze flat and strange. *The gaze of a dead snake.*

"I know you know," he says quietly, almost whispering, his voice as flat and strange as the look in his eyes. The overly calm tone is enraging – he has no right to be calm.

"You have no idea what I know!"

"I know you know I'm not an official investigator on this case," he says, still with the same flat tone.

"You're not anything on this case! You're a nobody!"

He slowly pulls away and settles into the armchair, almost sinking into it. Only now do I pause to sweep my gaze across the apartment, which is awash with a glaring light and sharp angles. It looks very new. Too new. Everything around us is glowing with surgical sterility, and there's not a single personal item in the place apart from a giant wall clock, polished white, its enormous second hand sweeping across the dial. *Tick-tock, tick-tock.*

Micha is still fixed to the armchair, looking like a wax figure lifted from the museum. Staring into space in a spectacular display of indifference, he ignores my presence, as if all at once he just stopped caring, or maybe he could only get his groove on when he was lying and pretending to be someone else. *He looks like he's mourning something. Someone.*

"I'm a volunteer in the detective division," he says as if that explains everything.

"A volunteer? So how did you get access to all that information?" I want to kill him, pummel him with my bare hands, rip him apart, tear off the cloak of indifference, sully this clean, impersonal apartment, which looks uninhabited. Although I can sense he lives here, that he's exactly the type to leave no trace behind. Unlike me, with my breadcrumb trail wherever I go, for the children who'll never follow…

"Sheila, relax," he says, and I have to wonder whether there's a single person on the planet who ever responded well to that directive, let alone actually relaxed.

"Relax?" I almost scream. *Scream, scream.*

"My uncle is Amiram Yarden." When he sees my blank expression, he adds, "The precinct commander."

"So the illustrious commander is okay with fraud?"

His rapid blinking gives him away.

"Ah, so he doesn't know?" I jeer. "He doesn't know what a lying loser his volunteer nephew is?"

Shut up, you won't get anything this way, shut your trap already, do a clean job and get what you want out of him.

But shouting feels oh-so-good, so freeing. I realize how much I've been holding back in his presence, how hard I've been trying to be everything I'm not, everything I thought he wanted me to be, so much so that I made up some kind of ghost-Sheila that doesn't exist. And since he came up with a fictional character for himself, I guess you could say we're two peas in a fake pod. *Or maybe four peas.*

I look up at the wall clock and notice that the giant hands resemble two sharp knives, and the second hand a thin scalpel spinning much too fast. *Tick-tock, tick-tock.*

"He knew I was involved in the investigation in my own way," he notes with carefully chosen words, "I had his unspoken consent."

We stare at each other again. Even with his body sunken in the soft white armchair, he still manages to look tall and straight-backed. I picture the boy who was ensnared in a back brace that forced him into sitting like this. *Now he doesn't need to be forced, the body has learned its lesson; there's nothing the body doesn't remember.*

"And why would the precinct commander allow you to meddle in the investigation in such an ugly way?"

The second hand keeps spinning at full tilt, the tiny scalpel trapped between the two knives. *Tick-tock, tick-tock, tick-tock.*

"I think you know why," he says very quietly.

Tick-tock, tick-tock, tick-tock.

He's right, of course. In a way, I knew from the very first moment. Turns out I knew a lot of things. Good witches never lose their powers; they just decide sometimes that they're better off not knowing; they know that in certain cases, living in denial is better than the alternative.

"How long were you together, you and Dina?" I ask, feeling my lungs slowly fill with water. "How long?"

While waiting for an answer, I remember how in every interview, Dina always took pride in the fact that "when it comes to men, I have a strict, casual, short-and-sweet policy," and I know that if it turns out that he, of all people, was the one who got her to break that policy, it'll hurt.

"Only a few months," he says. But it still hurts, because I hear that naked pining in his voice, that note that sounded in our very first meeting, when he told me, "my girlfriend was your age," and even back then, *even back then!*, I detected a distant, dim echo coming off his words, but I chose not to listen, and it may have even made me want to get closer. And there were also those little moments when I could feel his admiration – excessive, in my opinion – for her, and when I felt the tiny pang of jealousy, I convinced myself it was just my regular Dina envy, but deep down I knew something else lay there, deeper and darker. *The Others will always recognize each other.* And as with the feeling of lurking danger, this too made me want to get closer to him.

Didn't I already tell you you're a stupid baby? Dina's voice whispers in my ear again, but I'm not listening to her, I know she's wrong. I was never stupid, I just chose not to be smart, and while some choices are irreversible, this one I can change in a wink.

"You were the father of her baby?"

Tick-tock, tick-tock.

His eyes fill with pain.

No tot, no tot.

"No chance," he says, "she broke up with me more than a year ago."

Of course she's the one who broke it off; Dina isn't someone who gets dumped, Dina isn't someone who gets ghosted after sex. *Right now Dina is someone who's dead, so you can ease off a little.*

"So who was the father?" I ask.

"I don't know."

"And who's the killer?"

Tick-tock, tick-tock, tick-tock.

"Don't know that either."

But I do. And I know it's not you, it could never have been you: because it's a few sizes too big on you, because you're just a little boy who happened to stumble into a grown-up's world, because I find it ridiculous to even think Dina was into you, *and that you yourself were?* Because even this conversation, which should be dripping with drama, is plain boring. Because you're boring, sitting here, a little boy in a wife beater, an empty shell of self-importance.

"So you have no idea who the father could be?"

"I think she went to a sperm bank. And I'm telling you, sometimes the sperm bank is probably best for everyone."

A small, bitter smile appears on his face, and his hand reaches for his tattoo. "You know Dina was the one who suggested I get this tattoo? She knew the story about my dad."

I look at him as he launches into a long monologue about an emotionally absent father and a hard-knock life, and I wonder why he's telling me all this. Why now, when it's all over? He's sitting in front of me, going on and on, a diatribe full of rage and accusations against his father, with a passion that's usually reserved for the early days of a relationship, especially if he's the younger partner and you're there to play "understanding adult," even if we never played that game, thank God, and he's still holding forth, and I can't help but think how it *always* goes back to the starting point, the scene of the crime, the source of the genes, to what will be passed on from generation to generation; what is crooked can never be straightened. *Never!*

"You know that tattoo of yours is a commonly misconstrued verse," I cut him off in the middle of his sob story. "That sentence actually ends with a question mark. It's 'The fathers have eaten sour grapes, and the children's teeth are set on edge?' The children are *not* supposed to pay for the sins of their fathers." *Or mothers.*

"I know, Dina explained it to me," he says, again with that yearning in his voice, "she was the smartest person I knew."

I look at him and wonder whether I'll ever stop feeling that prick of jealousy whenever someone praises her, and realize it's probably just a matter of time. *Tick-tock, sometimes it can actually work in your favour.*

"You see, my father is a sorry excuse for a human being, and this tattoo makes sure I never forget that." He strokes his arm slowly, with lustful rapacity. It's a spine-chilling gesture.

"Fortunately, my uncle was there to save me," he adds.

"The precinct commander?"

"Yeah, I owe him everything."

"And what will the illustrious commander say when he hears about what you did to me?"

"What did I do to you?" He's not playing coy, he genuinely thinks he did nothing wrong and I'm just being dramatic. I feel like knocking him off his armchair and kicking him so hard he'll need that back brace again.

"You tricked me! You lied!" *You had sex with me, you left!*

"Oh, come on, Sheila, you're a smart person." I keep myself from asking if I'm "Dina smart," and he goes on, "She talked about you a lot, Dina, and at first I thought there was a chance you did it. Although I have to say, the moment you opened the door, I knew it wasn't you."

He says this as if he's disappointed in me, that he thought less of me once he learned I wasn't someone capable of murder. Although neither is he. Look at him sitting there, fondling his inane tattoo, eyeing me with self-satisfaction, when God only knows what he could possibly be satisfied about.

"What are you looking at?" he asks.

"I'm looking at an overgrown baby who's pleased with himself, even though he has zero reason to be."

Yes, it's definitely liberating. He seems surprised, and for a moment even insulted, but then he narrows his eyes and leans in, smiling, and says with an almost friendly tone, "So just for the record, and so you won't leave here empty-handed, you should know that Ronit Akiva was also undergoing some very intensive IVF treatments." When he notices my expression withering, he adds, "So Dina wasn't the only one who wanted to become a mother. Turns out that in the end, they all want to become mothers; I mean, all the normal women do, so what does that say about you?"

25

MY LEGS ARE SHAKING but I keep walking. *Dina wasn't the only one, Ronit wanted it too.*

He obviously meant to hurt me with that, Micha, meant and succeeded, *Ronit too!* But it'll take me some time to feel the full impact of that blow; right now my mind is racing with other thoughts, old insights, a muffled realization kicking and screaming inside me, trying to get out, Ronit was also undergoing IVF. *Intensive treatments. Ronit too!*

I recall the party at Ronit's, with Eli, all that crying, the mixed messages, running hot one moment and cold the next; it all makes sense now, as do her red eyes and that eerie whisper to me at the end of the party about her "last birthday." She probably meant it was going to be her last birthday as one of the Others. By her next one, she'd be like everyone else.

It's all turning upside down. I pick up my pace, *hurry, hurry!*

The realization sinks in deeper with every step I take: Dina and Ronit weren't murdered because they didn't want to be mothers, they were murdered for exactly the opposite reason; they were murdered because they *wanted* to be, they yearned for it, but someone out there decided it wasn't going to happen, decided these women had to live with the choices they made long ago, and once they wanted something else, that someone made them pay for it.

*

When that someone opens the door for me, I hear the sound of running water coming from the bathroom. It's a slow, menacing burble.

So this is what she has in store for me? The witch test? My senses perk up.

"You're early," she says. With her auburn hair carefully combed and her smooth, fresh face, she looks like a little girl. *Make no mistake, she's not your little munchkin any more.*

She signals me to follow her into her room. I immediately notice that Jezebel's cage is empty. A salty, metallic scent of blood still lingers in the air, bludgeoning my nostrils. *Blood for blood.*

"I finally discovered who sent you that picture of the witch," she says.

"Who?" I ask dutifully, like a mother playing a very private game with her baby, trying to mollify her in a world whose rules no one understands but them.

"Guess," she says with a sly grin.

"I really don't know."

"Neria Grossman." Noticing the disbelief in my eyes, she adds, "You don't believe me, do you?"

Holding up her phone to my face, she shows me a text sent to her: "*The number is registered under the name Neria Grossman*. Remember I did you a favour, and don't tell anyone who you got this from!"

Her small face beams with a proud smile.

"You could have faked that text too."

"Oh, please," she scoffs, "why would I want to frame that idiot, Neria?"

"Maybe to shake me up?"

"If I wanted to shake you up, I'd go for Micha," she says. "By the way, I hope you know he was never into me, not even for a moment." Now she sounds like a young woman trying to comfort the spurned spinster, but maybe she's right. Maybe Micha wasn't into her because of her tight black dress, maybe he was suspicious of her and that's why he was so eager to get her over to my place. *But why are you even thinking about that idiot now? He doesn't exist! He's not who he claimed to be, and maybe Neria Grossman isn't who you think he is either? You were never good at choosing your love interests, were you?*

"Where's Jezebel?" I ask.

"Dead," she replies.

Like everyone else who wanted to become a mother.

She approaches the empty cage and stands in front of it, and like last time, her hunched, thin back and slouched shoulders tug at my heart.

"You want the cage?" she asks. "You look like the pet hamster type."

I know she's trying to be cruel, but for some reason the remark makes me laugh, and while I can't see her face, I can feel her smiling. Chemistry is a very mysterious thing. *And it can be just as dangerous.*

"Gali, I know."

"So you want the cage or not?" she asks without turning to me.

"I *know*."

Still without turning to me, she presses her face against the empty cage.

"So what, you came to punish me?"

I'd never punish you, my little munchkin, and you know that. Who wants a cuddle from her Sheila? I waited and waited, and here you are, you came.

"No," I reply, "I came to help you."

Finally, she turns to me, once again her face wearing a child's innocence. I wonder if that was how Dina saw her too, when she invited her to the meeting that sealed her fate. *A child really does change the course of your destiny.*

I picture the pregnant Dina, the baby inside her sprouting limbs and growing bigger with every passing day, as she sits in her office making a list of all the people she wants to "clear the air" with. She was always so methodical, so punctilious. I was on that list, of course, only she didn't get to ask for my forgiveness because the conversation took an ugly turn too fast.

But I'm guessing that's nothing compared to the way her conversation with Gali escalated.

"She'd called you, hadn't she?" I ask. "Wanted to ask for your forgiveness, to apologize."

Gali isn't blinking, and I wonder if that's how she was with Dina, a childlike face masking a cold and calculating mind. Little children can't stay little forever. Dina saw her as Naama's daughter, and couldn't imagine that sometimes little girls grow up to wreak big havoc.

"What did she have to apologize for?" Again with the childish voice, but the look in her eyes tells me she knows exactly what Dina had to apologize for, that she had already considered the plea, decided it was too late for repentance and executed the verdict. I also know this might be the moment I should start being afraid.

That last night... the last night we were all alive... Thrump! Thrump! Give it up for all the original members of the Others!

This isn't a reunion, but it feels like one. We graduated a while ago and while Dina, Ronit and I still keep in contact, the friendship has wavered. However, since this is the pre-WhatsApp era, we make a point of meeting up every so often.

Naama is a whole other story. She's sitting there as still as a statue in the living room of Dina's new apartment, a cup of punch in her hand and an emptiness in her eyes.

That emptiness scares Dina and Ronit, who haven't seen her in a long time, but I'm not surprised by this two-and-a-half-year-old depression, only saddened.

"Is she seeing a therapist?" Dina whispers to me. "Getting some kind of professional help?"

I explain to her that Naama won't hear of it, but I don't tell her that the person who objects to the idea even more vociferously is Avihu, *There's nothing wrong with my wife.*

"It's just a case of mild depression that'll go away," I say and feel like an idiot, since Naama looks like a zombie. I want to explain to Dina that in her day-to-day, Naama is doing much better. It's true that she hasn't bounced back entirely, but that's probably normal when you're a mother to twin toddlers full of energy, especially that cute Gali, who looks like a miniature version of Naama.

But this whole get-together proves to be a bad idea. From the moment Naama walked in, she was slowly sapped of what little vitality she still had. Dina didn't spare her the snide digs we always made at each other, but I guess there are things you can say only when you're in daily contact, and once the relationship is no longer close, they aren't received well. Especially remarks like "So, Naama, still dreaming big?"

Thrump! Thrump! Thrump! The tambourine suddenly appears out of nowhere, and Dina starts pounding away.

"Remember how much fun we had at the beach? Remember, Naama?" Dina provokes.

Remember, sure I remember. Dina and Ronit press their fingers together, *the old oath.* Naama isn't moving, her hand clasps her cup of punch and it seems as if it's filling up with blood, *finger to finger. Like that. Our young voices chant together perfectly in sync, "No one wants kids, and no one needs kids, and we'll never ever have them, n-e-v-e-r!"*

Naama's eyes are empty. What's going on there, behind that hollow gaze? I know she doesn't regret the twins. "They're my everything," she told me more than once, and I believed her.

I want to believe her now too, but I can't.

Dina smells blood. "So, Naama, how's life treating you? What about all those great ambitions?"

Naama doesn't reply, and I want to tell Dina to shut her pie-hole. She's standing there with her tambourine without realizing how ridiculous she looks, and starts lecturing us about everything she'll do one day, and all the things she has already achieved, an action plan for a dazzling future. As she stands tall in the middle of the living room, holding forth, I look at her and think to myself, not for the first time, how self-involved and callous she is, this Dina. While that callousness may help her get ahead now, one day it'll be her downfall.

Naama continues to stare into space, her hands now peeling an apple she plucked from the fruit bowl. She's holding a small fruit knife, peeling the apple in one long ribbon.

I look at the swirling skin and recall reading somewhere that people once used apple peels to tell fortunes. You had to throw the peel onto the floor and the letter it formed was the first initial of your future husband's name. *But Naama already married Avihu, so what future is she uncoiling for herself there?*

And Dina, as if reading my mind, laughs at her, "So, how's motherhood? Already earned a PhD in pee-pee and poo-poo? Making good headway on the thesis about teething and that essay exploring butt wipes?"

I want to say something, but just then Naama replies very quietly, "There's more to life than academia, Dina. Being a mother is so much more… more fulfilling, it fills you with…" Her voice trails off and the long ribbon of apple peel falls onto the floor with a light tap. She doesn't look at it.

Dina smiles. "I don't know what it could possibly fill you with, Princess, other than maybe regret. So why don't you admit it?"

Then she turns to us. "Isn't it obvious that it's the worst thing she could have done with her life?"

I can't describe what followed without using the words frenzy and amok. Because Naama, the same Naama who sat swathed in her zombie-like silence all evening, lunged at Dina with the sharp fruit knife gleaming in her hand, passed by her and pierced the blade over and over again into the painting of Miriam the prophetess, who was watching us the entire night with a smile. *That smile!*

Ronit and I stood there stupefied, trying to calm her down but to no avail, and when Naama turned to Ronit with the knife still in her hand, Ronit punched her in the chest, hard. I jumped in and pulled Ronit off her and Naama staggered and fell to the floor, holding her aching hand, her face twisting with pain.

Then there was the mute ride home, Naama and I alone in the car with a veil of silence covering us like a dark and thick blanket. When we reached her house, she said, "Don't come in with me, I'll be fine," and gave me a small, reassuring smile.

I recalled that smile when they phoned me the next day to tell me that Naama had committed suicide, after trying to choke her little girls to death.

And now one of those little girls is standing in front of me, all grown up. The sound of running water coming from the bathroom becomes louder and I know that any moment now it's going to spill over the tub and flood the whole floor. *This is your swimming test! Don't fail!*

She considers me. "Don't worry," she says, and for a moment we switch roles and she's playing the mothering adult. "You'll pass the test. You're not pregnant and not planning to be."

Her voice is cold but her eyes are burning, and for the first time, I'm starting to question her sanity, even though deep down I know this little munchkin is perfectly sane in her own crazy way, and that if I walk out of here alive, she might end up behind bars. I start feeling that tug in my heart.

"Gali, let me help you – help me understand…"

"So that's what you want? The big confession, like in the books?" She takes a step closer to me and I flinch. "Trust me, you don't want that. The killer usually confesses to his next victim when he knows he won't be talking any more. It always seemed so ridiculous to me."

The loud gurgling sound takes on a new, splashing quality, and I realize the water has finally filled the tub and started to cascade onto the floor.

"But why?" are the only words I manage to produce.

"Why?" Gali blares. "Why? That fat Dina sat in her fancy office telling me how she always felt *uneasy*, and that she wants to *clear the air*, and then her face starts beaming and she tells me she's pregnant, *she's* pregnant! She gave my mother hell about it, my mother is dead because of her and now she's going to be a mother? No fucking way! And she has the audacity to tell me that it's *the natural state*, and that *eventually everybody wants to become a mother*, and look, even Ronit is trying! The whole gang from college, and *how exciting*, and she's telling me all this with an ecstatic expression, as if her being pregnant somehow fixes everything, as if *I* should be happy! My mum's six feet under and this heifer suddenly decides to calve, and she's telling me this with a smile!"

I can see it, Dina's smug, obtuse smile, the smile that eventually brought about her own death. Now it's Gali who's smiling, but it's a very different kind of smile.

"When my mother hanged herself with the tefillin straps, who do you think she was sending a message to?"

I keep my mouth shut.

"My poor dad, you know where he is right now? He went to visit her grave. He's there all the time. Because the tefillin were his, he thought in the beginning that she was trying to tell him something. It took him time to connect the dots, even though she told him everything that night when she came home, crying."

You should have gone in with her.

"He asked the police to make it go away; he said he did it for me, so the scandal would die down. He told me the truth only years later. He finally realized that she was talking to *you*, to the *Others* through Michal's tefillin, but her message didn't reach you, did it?! So when Dina told me about her pregnancy, I knew it was time my mother's message got through."

Gali falls silent and searches my face for the impact of her words.

Well, I just got the famous "confession," but I don't feel that sense of deep satisfaction described in all the detective stories. All I feel is sadness.

"It was easy after that. I called her and told her I wanted to meet up again, that I was doing a memorial video about my mother, and it was smooth sailing from there." Her eyes are shining, with an eerie sparkle.

"Don't tell me," I say.

"No problem, although I think you'd enjoy hearing it." And again with that conspiratorial smile, she continues, "I knew what I was going to do, it was so clear. My mum used Michal's tefillin? So Dina would get Miriam's tambourine, and Ronit would get Lilith's baby, and they'd both become the mothers they so wanted to be, just like they deserved."

A sudden chill creeps up my body, and I look down to discover the water has gushed out of the bathroom and is already wetting my feet. "Gali, what are you doing?"

"Stop being so afraid. I don't understand how a coward like you had the courage not to become a mother," she says and takes a step closer to me. *It's not courage, Gali, it's fear. It's the fear that buried all the other fears beneath it. Not the fear of death, but the fear of life.*

I turn to the door but find it locked; when did she lock it? I start shaking the door handle with growing hysteria. *Get out of here, now!* I look back in panic, and she's smiling at me. "It's just jammed."

I press down on the handle with all my might, and the door opens. *Out! Get out of here! Thrump! Thrump!*

Feet plodding through the water, I run to the bathtub and turn off the faucets. Finally, quiet. With all this water around me.

The water in the tub looks clear and inviting as I stand there, staring. Is this what the witches felt moments before they drowned? A kind of inner peace and desire to accept the invitation? To escape all that noise outside. *The water is calling you.*

I can feel Gali behind me, moving quickly and quietly, and suddenly I can see her movements during the murder with complete clarity, the small, efficient hand holding the knife. *The little girl who isn't a little girl. Who never was a little girl.* Oh, Naama, I'm glad you're not here to see this.

Facing each other, feet soaked in water, I look into her eyes and know what I need to do. *This time you're going to save this girl.*

"Gali, you need help."

"Help?" She laughs. "And who's going to help me, you?"

"I want to."

"You always want to help, you keep forgetting you're not my mum!"

No, I'm not. But I'm as disappointed and scared of you as if I were your mother.

I slip the knife I brought with me out of my pocket, because munchkin or no munchkin, I'm not taking any chances. I'm not going to end up with a baby doll glued to my hands.

"Oh, come on, Sheila!" She laughs again. "You're going to kill me? You?"

"I told you, I have no such intention, I just want to help you."

"Again with the helping me?" She steps closer to me, eyes flaming, *Thrump! Thrump! Thrump!* "Why don't I help *you*? Maybe

I'd be doing you a huge favour? So you won't end up an old spinster? So you won't die alone? Huh? What do you say? Will you let *me* help *you*?"

Now she's very close, and I'll never know if she actually wanted to lunge at me or if she just slipped in the water, but the next thing I know I feel a sharp blow and a tug, and all of a sudden there's a struggle over the knife, and I'm saying to myself, No, Sheila, this isn't happening to you, not you, with the quiet, sheltered life you designed for yourself; you went and shut yourself off from the outside world and its dangers, so how, for heaven's sake, are you standing here, in this bathroom, grappling over a knife with your little munchkin?

And the blood. Suddenly, there's blood everywhere. I don't feel any pain, but that might be the adrenaline. But then Gali collapses onto the floor, and I look at her and at the blood flowing, *so much blood.* It's mixing with the water and painting the floor blood-red, and I bend over and reach out to her but my hands are wet, and that nasty gash on her neck looks black and pulsing, and I try to press it to hold back all that blood, but my hands keep sliding, and I try and try, but it's all so sticky and slippery and red, *so red.*

No, she didn't say "mum" before she closed her eyes.

26

I'M CLEANING MY APARTMENT.

Ever since that fight with Micha, my hair had stayed resolutely on my head. No more clumps, so no more use for the special silicone broom. I put it on the balcony, amidst the pile of old junk. I keep the Witch of Endor painting there too. I still can't throw it away. But I'll get there eventually.

Gali survived, of course.

In the story I'm telling, Gali couldn't have died. I would never have let that happen. Besides, the EMS pre-arrival instructions were very clear. They also arrived surprisingly fast.

I recall the gushing blood, the dark pulses of life gradually leaving her body, recall the horrible fear that filled every part of me and can't help but think about Dina and Ronit.

Yes, eventually, Gali told me how she led them to their deaths. And she was right, I did want to hear the details. "You won't believe what you can find online nowadays," she said with that same brisk, matter-of-fact tone. "There's a manual for everything."

When she called them asking to meet, they immediately agreed, and how could they not? To them, she'd always be Naama's daughter. And their guilt must have numbed any inkling of suspicion.

In our meeting, so she told me, still with that same flat tone, she put crushed sleeping pills in their drinks. When the pills kicked in and they became drowsy, she tied them to the armchairs, and slashed their femoral arteries. She told me how she sat and watched the blood flow, and hinted that she collected it in a large vessel. She didn't tell me what she did with all that blood, but I have my theories.

Ronit was suspicious. Liliths always are. At the last minute, when she was already too sleepy to resist, she looked straight into Gali's eyes and knew what was going to happen to her. And more importantly, she understood the reason for it.

Gali told me that the look in her eyes was enough for her. "Maybe if Dina had looked at me the same way, with genuine regret and sadness, I wouldn't have had to kill Ronit too," she said. But Dina, as I've mentioned, never could apologize. Even when she wanted to.

I sometimes wonder about the child she would have had, Dina, if he would have looked like her, what kind of person he would have grown up to be, but I always shoo those thoughts away.

By the way, Gali wasn't lying when she told me the picture of the drowned witch was sent to me from Neria Grossman's phone, but the person who sent it was Taliunger, who took Frida Gotteskind's witches course with us.

Obviously, she'd never admit it, Tali, and for now I have no intention of wringing a confession out of her, but I still get a kick out of knowing.

And Shirley's pregnant, walking around the museum all peaceful and pretty.

When she asked me if I wanted to touch her belly, I hesitated for a moment but then reached out. Her stomach was spongy and throbbing, and when I told Gali about it, it made her laugh.

Eli is still a bit mad that I didn't share my suspicions with him, but I'm sure he'll get over it soon. We know each other so well that he knows exactly why I disappeared on him these past few weeks. He's also the only one who understands my daily visits with Gali.

Yes, I visit her every day.

The guards have already gotten used to me. Even Avihu is used to it by now, and says I'm a good influence on her. I wonder what he would think if I told him it's actually the other way around.

"She so waits for your visits," he says.

He has no idea how much *I* wait for them.

Because that's how it is when a baby calls out to you from the darkness, and a girl is waiting for you on the other side of a tall wall.

Apparently, there are all kinds of relationships. All kinds of love.

ABOUT THE AUTHOR AND TRANSLATOR

SARAH BLAU is an author and playwright, a recipient of the 2015 Prime Minister's Prize for Hebrew Literary Works, and the 2017 Bar-Ilan University Alumni Achievement Award in recognition of her contribution to enriching culture in Israel and her activity in the fields of literature and communication. She currently lives in Tel Aviv. An international bestseller, *The Others* is her American debut novel.

Born in Israel in 1983, DANIELLA ZAMIR is a literary translator of contemporary Israeli fiction. She obtained her bachelor's degree in literature from Tel Aviv University, and her master's degree in creative writing from City University in London. She currently lives in Tel Aviv with her sort-of-husband and two cats.